COMEDY OF ERRORS

By the time Todd and Ron walked away, still snickering, Stephanie was convinced that Derek was working on a way to ditch her. Why would he want to spend the rest of the evening with the laughingstock of Oakmont High?

Derek's voice interrupted her thoughts. "Want to dance?"

Well, apparently he hadn't decided to ditch her yet.

He led her onto the dance floor and pulled her into his arms, linking his hands around her waist. Stephanie's arms encircled his neck, and their eyes locked. Waves of delight flooded Stephanie's senses as Derek moved closer. And then he kissed her.

In that instant, Stephanie realized she was falling in love with Derek Gaines. She closed her eyes, wishing the song would go on forever.

Bantam Sweet Dreams romances
Ask your bookseller for the books you have missed

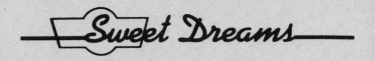

COMEDY OF ERRORS

Diane Michele Crawford

BANTAM BOOKS

NEW YORK · TORONTO · LONDON · SYDNEY · AUCKLAND

RL 6, age 11 and up

COMEDY OF ERRORS
A Bantam Book / October 1992

Sweet Dreams and its associated logo are registered trademarks of Bantam Books, a division of Bantam Doubleday Dell Publishing Group, Inc. Registered in U.S. Patent and Trademark Office and elsewhere.

Cover photo by Pat Hill

ISBN 0-553-29457-1

Published simultaneously in the United States and Canada

Bantam Books are published by Bantam Books, a division of Bantam Doubleday Dell Publishing Group, Inc. Its trademark, consisting of the words "Bantam Books" and the portrayal of a rooster, is Registered in U.S. Patent and Trademark Office and in other countries. Marca Registrada. Bantam Books, 666 Fifth Avenue, New York, New York 10103.

PRINTED IN THE UNITED STATES OF AMERICA

OPM   0 9 8 7 6 5 4 3 2 1

Chapter One

"Slow down, Missy," Stephanie Stockwell said, trying to keep up with her friend. "Why are you in such a big hurry to get to study hall?"

"I need some books from my locker," Missy explained, without slowing her brisk pace through the crowded halls of Oakmont High. "My history report is due tomorrow, and I haven't even started it."

Stephanie couldn't believe her ears. "You're going to *study*? You're going to break our tradition of *not* doing homework during study period?"

Someone bumped into Missy before she could answer. Losing her balance, she grabbed for Stephanie's arm. Together they careened into a bank of lockers.

1

Stephanie unexpectedly found herself with one foot wedged awkwardly inside an open gym bag, her shoelace snagged on something as she tried twisting free. Since groping in a stranger's gym bag didn't seem right, Stephanie looked around for the owner and found herself staring at one very broad letterman-jacketed back. The guy was too busy talking to some of his friends to even notice her.

She glanced at Missy, who tilted her head toward the expanse of shoulders next to Stephanie. "Todd Cooper," she whispered.

"Great," Stephanie muttered. Todd Cooper was, without a doubt, the greatest-looking member of the Oakmont High Cougars football team. She'd die before she'd tap him on one of his gorgeous shoulders, begging for release from his gym bag. But the alternatives included being stuck until he noticed. Then he'd think she was weird.

"Steph!" Missy pointed to the time.

Stephanie took a deep breath. Todd was starting to walk away—it was now or never. "Todd!" she yelled.

Startled, he turned around and stared at her.

"Uh . . . um . . . I . . . your . . ." Stephanie stammered, pointing to her foot, while her face grew hotter and hotter. "Jaws is alive and well at Oakmont High," she said weakly.

Her attempt at humor was rewarded immediately by a gorgeous smile from Todd Cooper. "Need some rescuing?" he asked, moving to her side. Todd's aquamarine eyes held hers momentarily before he moved on to the business at hand. "I forgot I left this here."

Stephanie babbled an apology and explained her captivity while Todd concentrated on untangling her shoe.

"There you go," he said when Stephanie's foot came free at last.

She wiggled her foot back and forth a couple of times. "Nothing seems to be missing."

Missy rolled her eyes. "Only a few brain cells. Come on, Steph, we'll be late."

"Thanks for the help," Stephanie said over her shoulder, hastily following Missy.

After making a quick stop at Missy's locker for her history book, the girls raced through the library door to their assigned study hall table as the final bell was ringing.

Wasting no time, Stephanie got right to work. She flipped open her spiral notebook to a blank page. Next to her, Missy spread out binders and books. Paper ripping away from its binding momentarily interrupted the silent library. Stephanie glanced up and caught Mr. Osterman's look of disapproval.

That man should work for the CIA, she scribbled on the sheet of lined paper in front of her. *He hears everything*. She folded the note and slid it to Missy.

They had mastered "Undetected Note Passing 1-A," as Stephanie phrased their skill, when they were still in junior high. The trick required sitting like a zombie, with both elbows on the table. While giving the illusion of studying, the note was placed under one elbow. The elbow inched toward the partner's elbow waiting to cover the exposed part of the note and take possession as the sender's elbow rushed back into awaiting-answer position.

Stephanie turned a page of her Spanish book to convince Mr. Osterman she was studying. She looked up to see if he was patrolling, but instead met a pair of amused blue eyes across the table.

Derek Gaines watched her for a moment before turning his attention back to his studies. Derek actually did his homework during sixth period!

According to Missy, who loved using her position as second period office assistant to snoop in student files, Derek was a senior, out-of-state transfer student. Stephanie and Missy had decided that he was much too serious, though he wasn't bad looking at all.

Now Missy passed a note. *Todd will always remember how the blue of his gym bag contrasted with your white tube socks!*

You're such a romantic! Stephanie wrote back. *I'm totally humiliated. I made a fool out of myself, all red-faced and stammering!*

But Steph, you know how red emphasizes your big, brown eyes! Missy responded.

Stephanie giggled out loud, causing Mr. Osterman to scowl. Derek Gaines stared at her, and she quickly hid behind her Spanish book, ignoring Derek the Spy, a nickname she and Missy had made up.

The two girls had been best friends since second grade, when they had convinced their classmates that they were twins, separated at birth and adopted by two different families. Being *fraternal* twins explained Stephanie's brown hair, brown eyes, and below-average height, and

Missy's blond hair, blue eyes, and above-average height.

I can't hang around after school today, Missy wrote. *Good ol' Chuck is driving me to the city library for research material for this history paper. I'd offer you a ride home, but you know Chuck.*

Stephanie was well aware of how Missy's older brother would react to taking her home, in the opposite direction of the library. He was a senior who considered lower classmen, especially sophomores, barely one step above aliens.

Finally the bell rang, and the girls gathered their books.

"Did you remember to sign up for the Collegiennes?" Missy asked. "Today's the last day."

"I'll do it after school," Stephanie promised. The Collegiennes was a school-sponsored service organization whose members tutored elementary grade children in reading and math.

"Stephanie!" a voice called out. She turned to see Derek Gaines walking toward them.

"Oh, great!" she moaned. "What could he possibly want?"

"Call me later with the sordid details," Missy said, edging out into the hallway.

Stephanie watched her disappear down the hall into the throng of students.

"I'm glad I caught you," Derek announced. He shifted his armload of books and handed her the top one. "You forgot your Spanish book," he said smiling. "You spend so much time studying Spanish, I figured you'd be lost without it."

So! In between trigonometry and French IV, Derek the Spy had observed her study habits.

"See you later," he said.

Stephanie raised her hand in a half wave and headed off to seventh period English, wondering about Derek Gaines. He was actually cute when he smiled. Not in the fantastic category like Todd, but still, not bad. . . .

After school Stephanie hurried to the Administration building and signed up for the Collegiennes. Above the roster was a notice of their first scheduled meeting during lunch the next day. She jotted down the information and left the building, heading for home.

Mrs. Stockwell was already buckling the baby into the car seat when Stephanie walked up the driveway. "The twins helped themselves to at least a half dozen chocolate chip cookies each while I was getting Stacey ready for her checkup, so food in any way, shape, or form is off-limits for them until dinnertime." She got in the driver's side of the car. "Thanks, Steph." She blew her oldest daughter a kiss and drove off.

When Stephanie walked inside, she saw her eight-year-old twin sisters sitting peacefully at the kitchen counter.

"What's going on?" she asked, removing the chocolate chip cookies from each of their hands.

"Hey!" Shannon protested, her freckled face scowling identically to the mirror image sitting next to her.

"Mom said no more food until dinner. Now what's going on?"

Sarah's dark eyes lit up. "We're rehearsing for our play."

"*My* play, you mean," Shannon corrected.

Stephanie set her books on the counter. "I haven't heard anything about a play."

"I'm writing this really scary play about monsters and ghosts," Shannon explained excitedly. "Dad said we could use the garage and invite everyone like last time."

Sarah chimed in, "There's even a part for you." Both twins giggled. "You're the storyteller . . . and you happen to be a witch."

8

Stephanie rolled her eyes. "Gee, thanks."

"But you get turned into a regular person at the end," Shannon added. "If I can figure out how."

"You'll love the makeup, Steph," Sarah promised. "Your face is going to be yucky green, and we're going to glue a black wart on your nose."

"Charming," Stephanie murmured under her breath, but the twins were already bounding out of the room, chattering about their plans.

Chapter Two

Stephanie and Missy settled into seats near the front of the auditorium the next day during the noon break.

Bonnie Kramer, president of the Collegiennes, introduced herself and the other club officers, then explained about the group. "The main focus of the Collegiennes is tutoring elementary-school-age kids. We appreciate your joining our organization. There are a lot of kids who need our help."

Bonnie pointed to the auditorium entrance. "We have two tables set up in the foyer. One has personal information forms for you to fill out. Be sure to let us know if you'd like to tutor a student in math or reading. We'll make assignments and call you over the weekend.

"On the other table are some handouts we've prepared: some simple guidelines and suggestions to start you off, and a Collegienne roster with officer and member phone numbers that we'll update in the next month or so after all our new members have settled in." She consulted a small notebook. "Our regular meetings are held once a month on campus."

Bonnie motioned toward the other club officers and added, "We'll be glad to answer any questions while you're filling out your forms."

"I think I'd like tutoring someone in reading," Stephanie told Missy as they went out into the foyer. She loved to read and couldn't imagine her own life without the special worlds she discovered in books.

"Me, too," Missy said, reaching for a couple of information sheets.

Stephanie finished her forms as the warning bell signaled the end of lunch period. "I'll see you later in study hall," she told Missy, who was still filling out her information sheet.

Biology was Stephanie's first class after lunch. Earlier that day she'd caught a glimpse of Todd's back as he rummaged around in his locker. Now, as she hurried past, not looking where she was going, she ran straight into him!

"I'm sorry," she muttered as she looked up into Todd's amused face. She wondered ruefully if their conversations would ever start off without an apology from her.

Todd gave her one of his heart-stopping smiles. "No problem." He laughed. "Been attacked by any woman-eating gym bags lately?"

Stephanie's face flushed as she shook her head and forced a casual grin. "Yours seems to be the only hungry one around."

Todd draped an arm loosely around her shoulders. "That grimy gym bag must be trying to tell me something."

Stephanie just giggled nervously.

"How about going to the game and the dance with me on Friday?" Todd suggested.

Stephanie was stunned. The game and the dance with *Todd Cooper*? She must be dreaming! What had happened to Jessica What's-Her-Name, the redhead she'd seen him with last week? Or was last week Ashley Bennett? What difference did it make, anyway? If Todd wanted her to be Miss First Week of October, who was she to deny him?

Todd didn't bother waiting for her answer. He'd probably never been turned down by a female in his entire life. "I'll pick you up around six-thirty. We can catch some of the junior varsity game, then I'll need to suit up." He leaned closer. "You'll have to cheer me on while we slaughter Ridgeway."

To be anywhere near Todd Cooper before, during, or after the slaughter, Stephanie would cheerfully have volunteered for a fifty-mile hike through the Sahara Desert, barefoot. "Thanks. I'd love to," she said at last.

"Great." He pulled her against his chest and reached behind her, yanking a scrap of paper out of the binder in his other hand. "Write down your phone number and address."

When he released her, Stephanie was quivering. She'd never been molded to a guy before, and it was making her very nervous. She pulled a pencil out of her purse, hoping he could decipher her shaky hieroglyphics.

"Better put your name down there, too," Todd added.

She stared at the paper he'd given her, feeling completely humiliated. Todd hadn't even bothered to find out her name! Then she looked up into that incredible face and instantly forgave him. "Stephanie Stockwell," she said, writing it down at the same time.

Todd took the paper from her. "Great." He patted her on the back. "See you."

Stephanie floated off to biology, hearing none of Ms. Harris's lecture on the human skeletal system. When that class ended, she raced to study hall, grabbing Missy's sleeve as she skidded to a halt inside the door. "You'll never in a trillion years guess what happened on the way to biology!"

Missy looked at her friend's flushed face and bright eyes. "Give me a hint and my usual three guesses," she said, heading for their study table.

Stephanie sat down. "The hint is Jaws."

"You're kidding!" Missy shrieked, dropping her books onto the table. "You fell into Todd's gym bag again?"

"No, but you're close."

"You fell into someone else's gym bag?"

"Way off." Stephanie opened a book, trying to look casual.

"*Todd* fell into someone else's gym bag!" was Missy's final guess.

Stephanie bent closer to her and whispered, "Todd Cooper asked me to the Friday night football game and dance!"

"Are you serious?" Missy gasped. She

pointed to the notebook in front of Stephanie. "Tell me *everything.*"

Stephanie giggled at the incredulous look on her friend's face and pulled a pencil out of her purse. For the next several minutes, she wrote fast and furiously, until Missy kicked her under the table. Derek Gaines was looking at her thoughtfully, tapping his chin with a pen. Didn't he have anything better to do than stare?

Missy impatiently nudged her. "If you're going to write a book, I'll wait for the movie," she whispered.

Stephanie quickly folded up the note and placed it in Missy's eager hand, watching while she devoured all the details and smiling at the astonished look on Missy's face.

How rude! Missy finally wrote back. *Todd didn't have the class to find out your name? Maybe the guy's a jerk.*

My feelings were a little hurt, Stephanie admitted on paper. *But you'd be surprised how easy it is to forgive someone as gorgeous as Todd.*

Maybe good looks aren't everything, Missy wrote back.

Ha! Look who's talking! Aren't you the same Marcia Elizabeth Franklin who nearly flunked algebra last semester be-

cause Simon Abercrombie sat in the front row? You spent the whole period drooling over him instead of paying attention!

Okay, okay. Guilty as charged. But at least Simon knows my name, Missy acknowledged by note.

Stephanie had just started writing her retort when the bell rang. "Saved by the bell," she said, gathering up her books.

As they headed for the door, Missy smiled wistfully. "You are *so* lucky! You and Todd Cooper. Does he have a fantastic-looking friend with a gym bag you can push me into?"

"*I'm* the Accident Queen." Stephanie closed her eyes and touched her forehead. "But because you're my best friend, I'm passing my powers on to you." She put her hand on Missy's forehead. "You now possess the gift of klutz, the ability to crash your way into gym bags and the hearts of gorgeous seniors, like Simon Abercrombie." Both girls laughed aloud.

When Stephanie got home from school, she checked in with her mom and then headed straight for her room. She spent the next few hours taking inventory of her wardrobe and fifteen minutes studying for an English test. Shortly before six, she went downstairs and set the table.

Dinnertime at the Stockwells' was always chaotic. This was the family's catching-up time. The days always started off on the hectic side, with too many people and too few bathrooms. Mr. Stockwell claimed the first shower, and by the time the girls had taken their turns he was on his way out the door to his job at the busy accounting firm of Lundquist and Lundquist. At supper, Stephanie's father made certain each of his daughters talked about her day.

By six-fifteen the family was all seated around the large oval dining table.

"So, how's the play coming along, girls?" their dad asked, tying a bib around Stacey's pudgy neck.

"Great!" Shannon answered as she passed the casserole dish to Stephanie.

"We're working on the end now," Sarah volunteered.

Stephanie waited for either twin to bring up their money-making scheme for the new production. "Don't you two have something to ask Dad?" she prompted.

Shannon stopped a forkful of green beans on its way to her mouth. "You mean about charging admission?"

Mrs. Stockwell laughed. "Chips off the old block, Mr. Accountant Stockwell!"

He said solemnly, "Girls, sometimes glory

is enough of a reward." Sarah and Shannon giggled. "I'm sure there are plenty of famous movie stars who started out doing plays for free in their garages."

"I'd rather be a famous writer," Sarah mused. "After being in my plays, Stephanie will be the movie star in the family."

Stephanie fluffed her hair in a mock dramatic gesture and batted her eyelashes. "My name will never be up in lights if you keep hiding all this beauty under tons of green goo and plastering fake warts on it."

Her mother gave Stephanie a sympathetic look. "Another witch role?"

"It's the best one yet," Shannon said enthusiastically. "We'll finish the story tonight, so we can practice tomorrow night and all day Saturday."

"Two days more than last time," Sarah added.

"Count me out for tomorrow night," Stephanie said quickly and then stopped.

"Why? What's tomorrow night?" Sarah asked.

"A guy asked me to go to the football game and the after-game dance with him," Stephanie answered, a little embarrassed.

Sarah moaned at the loss of valuable rehearsal time, but the wheels in Shannon's mind went into overdrive. "Then we'll just write in a part for him! You can both stay home and rehearse with us."

"That way," Sarah added, "you won't miss our Japanese dinner. We're going to dress Japanese and everything!"

"The girls are studying about Japan in school," Mrs. Stockwell explained to Stephanie, "and tomorrow night I'm cooking Japanese food." Turning to the twins, she said, "I'm afraid Stephanie's young man would rather be in the football stadium with a pretty girl than eating dinner Japanese-style and rehearsing as who-knows-what in your play."

Mr. Stockwell scraped the last bits of food out of Stacey's dish and made airplane noises before landing the spoon into her open mouth. "So tell us about the new guy in your life, Steph."

Stephanie blushed as she suddenly became the focus of the entire family.

"Is it 'Derek the Spy'?" Sarah asked.

"Derek the Spy?" Mrs. Stockwell repeated, obviously intrigued.

There were times when Stephanie wished she were an only child. "No, it's not, and the only way anyone would know that name is by eavesdropping on *private* phone conversations!"

Their mother looked sternly at the twins.

"Girls, I've told you before that Stephanie has a right to privacy. When she's on the phone, make yourselves scarce. Now you two can clear the table and rinse off the dishes while we finish talking."

"Aw, Mom," both twins whined as they stood up to accept the empty plate in her outstretched hand.

"So who is this 'Spy' person?" Mrs. Stockwell whispered to Stephanie when the twins left the room.

Mr. Stockwell looked amused. "What happened to our daughter's right to privacy?"

"I've protected Steph's *future* privacy by scolding the twins, but as long as this mysterious spy is out in the open, I'm curious."

" 'Derek the Spy' is Derek Gaines, a senior, who sits across the table from Missy and me in study hall," Stephanie explained. "We call him that because he's always watching us."

"Maybe he thinks you and Missy are cute," her mom said.

Stephanie shook her head. "We're way too goofy for Derek. I think he's allergic to giggling females."

Her father interjected, "Tell us about the boy you're going out with."

Stephanie beamed. "His name's Todd

Cooper, and he's a tall, blond, handsome football player. . . ."

The telephone rang. A second later one of the twins screeched her name from the kitchen.

"Take your call in the family room, Stephanie," her mother suggested, taking Stacey out of the high chair. "We'll supervise the overactive ears in the kitchen."

Stephanie flew out of the dining room into the cozy family room that was cluttered with Stacey's toys. Plopping down on the sofa, Stephanie took a few deep breaths before she dared pick up the receiver, thinking it was Todd. Her heart raced at the memory of his handsome face smiling at her earlier that day. At last she said, "Hello?"

"Hi, what's up?" It was Missy's familiar voice.

"Well, actually not much. I was hoping you were Todd."

Missy laughed. "Sorry to disappoint you. If you want me to clear the phone lines, just say the word."

"I can spare my best friend in the world approximately ten seconds," Stephanie teased.

"Great. This isn't why I'm calling, but I ran into Derek Gaines a while ago at

Ingram's Hardware Store. He works there," Missy said. "I felt like a total dweeb when I asked where the putty knives were and he pointed to a huge selection right in front of my nose!"

Stephanie groaned. "For someone who doesn't figure in my life, Derek Gaines took up fifteen whole minutes of dinner conversation. Now he's using up your ten seconds!"

"Okay, okay, I'll hurry." Missy took a loud intake of breath for Stephanie's benefit, and as fast as possible rattled off, "We're going to visit my aunt Celia so we're getting up at five A.M. on Saturday so I can't go to the game or the dance and I wanted to be there to watch you and Todd and live my love life vicariously through you." She gasped for air. "Even though he didn't know your name."

Stephanie convulsed with laughter. "If I forgave him, Missy, then you should, too."

"Only if you memorize every second of your date and tell me all the delicious details on Sunday night," Missy announced. "I want to find out how he stacks up against your previous boyfriends."

Stephanie feigned a coughing spasm. "*What* previous boyfriends? Tommy Anderson, that pest in third grade? Or Joe

Fletcher, whose mother bribed him into taking me to a sixth-grade dance because she and my mom were friends?"

"If I remember right, you and Tommy Anderson were a pretty hot item in third grade!" Missy teased.

Missy's brother, Chuck, broke into the phone conversation just then. "Time's up, girls. I'm expecting an important call."

Stephanie listened patiently to the garbled arguing at the Franklin house. Missy was the momentary winner. "How about taking my dad's video camera along with you tomorrow night? That way I won't miss a single minute of the big event."

"Good-bye, Stephanie," Chuck shouted into the phone. Before Stephanie had a chance to retort, the dial tone buzzed in her ear.

She replaced the receiver, then scrunched down on the sofa, resting her head on a cushion. Glancing at the wall clock, she decided there were still two or three acceptable calling hours left. There was still a chance that Todd might call.

"Steph!" a twin's voice yelled from several rooms away. "Your turn in the kitchen."

Stephanie looked down at the telephone and scowled. She knew that Todd was a busy guy, with daily football practice and homework. It was a hectic schedule with little time left for socializing on the phone, but the rationale didn't make her feel any better.

Chapter Three

The following evening, Stephanie carefully pulled the bulky knit sweater over her head and checked the French braid her mother had spent fifteen minutes perfecting. Not a hair out of place, thank goodness.

Smoothing the sweater over her jeans, Stephanie inspected her reflection in the full-length mirror beside her dresser. She turned a few times, critically examining herself from all angles.

"Casual but attractive," she thought aloud. "Warm enough for tonight's game and nice enough for the dance later."

According to Missy, this dusty-rose-colored sweater looked so good on Stephanie that Todd's days of dating Oakmont High's entire female student population were numbered. Stephanie wasn't expecting any miracles. "You have to be realistic," she told her reflection. "Enjoy one night of fun with a fantastic guy and don't expect anything more." Then she smiled. "On the other hand, maybe tonight's date will dazzle Todd into asking me out again." *Get back to reality, Stephanie,* she thought to herself.

She checked what little makeup she wore. Still as fresh as it had been when she'd checked three minutes earlier. Stephanie hadn't been this nervous since sixth grade when Joe Fletcher took her to the dance!

The sound of a car pulling into the driveway interrupted her thoughts. She moved away from the mirror and walked quickly to the window, feeling on the verge of an anxiety attack. From upstairs Stephanie could see the front half of Todd's red Toyota pickup right behind the family station wagon.

"Take a deep breath and relax," she instructed herself. Then the doorbell rang, jolting her heart rate off the charts, and she heard the dog barking.

The dog! Who let him in?

Stephanie raced out of her room, flying down the stairs at record speed. She screamed at Sarah, who was wearing her father's paisley pajama top with a bright red scarf tied around her waist and reaching for the door. "No!"

But it was too late. The front door swung open and Todd stood on the threshold looking tall and terrific. Spot, the Stockwells' oversized, overly affectionate dalmatian, had his huge front paws on Todd's chest, and he was licking the startled guest's face!

"I'm Sarah and that's Spot," the twin explained cheerfully.

"Get down, Spot!" Stephanie ordered, forcing a weak smile. There must have been a hint of desperation in her voice because for the first time in years, the dog responded instantly to her command.

"Hello," said a deep voice from the doorway leading to the dining room. Mr. Stockwell approached, dressed in a white karate outfit, and bowed at the waist. "Welcome to our humble home. I'm Papa Stockwell."

Stephanie laughed at the expression on Todd's face. She should have briefed him on her family, but his surprise was the price he had to pay for not phoning her before tonight.

"Todd, this is my father, Steven Stockwell. Dad, Todd Cooper."

Mr. Stockwell bowed once more before shaking Todd's reluctantly extended hand.

"The twins are studying Japan," Stephanie said, nodding her head toward the dining room where the rest of the family now stood. Each of them bowed in turn, grinning and saying, *"Sayonara."*

Mrs. Stockwell, in an authentic blue floral kimono, held Stacey in her arms. What had previously been a pillowcase was now Stacey's custom-made kimono, cinched at the waist with her favorite Mickey Mouse belt. Sarah stood next to Shannon, who wore what looked to Stephanie like a shortened version of Dad's old red terry cloth bathrobe.

Mr. Stockwell finished the introductions in his terrible Japanese accent, then turned to the still-bewildered Todd. "Too bad name Cooper," he said, shaking his head. "Have joyous time but be back to humble home by stroke of midnight."

Stephanie burst into laughter. "Dad, I think you're getting a little Cinderella mixed in with your Japanese." She took Todd by the hand and headed toward the door. Todd looked a bit dazed. "Nice meeting you," he mumbled, as several choruses of *Sayonara* accompanied them outside.

Stephanie was still giggling when Todd helped her into his pickup. "They may be a little strange," she said, "but you certainly can't accuse my family of being dull!"

"That's for sure," Todd muttered as he shut the door. There wasn't a trace of humor in his voice.

Stephanie watched him walk around to the driver's side, puzzled by the slight frown on his handsome face. Had she already done something wrong? Had her family done or said something wrong? Their Japanese theme wasn't *that* peculiar, was it?

Todd pulled out of the driveway. "What did your father mean about my name?"

His question sent a wave of relief through Stephanie. The explanation was bound to put a smile on Todd's face. "My parents are Steven and Susan Stockwell, and my sisters are Sarah, Shannon, and Stacey," she rattled off lightly as she had many times before. "Dad always jokes about all of us marrying guys whose last names begin with S to carry on the family tradition."

Todd continued frowning. "One date and your father thinks we're serious?"

Stephanie's face colored. "No, of course not! It's just his wacky sense of humor.

Sorry." Apologizing for her parents' behavior was a new experience, and one that made Stephanie uncomfortable.

She was relieved to see a grin on Todd's face. "No problem," he said, and swiftly changed the subject. "Did you see last week's game? We really slaughtered those guys from Lincoln!"

"Unfortunately, I was baby-sitting that night. But I went to the game before that, when we played Washington High."

Todd slapped his hand against the steering wheel. "I only played the first half—I wrenched my knee." He went on to explain numerous plays he'd made before the mishap, the plays leading up to it, and even a few of the plays after his injury.

Stephanie wasn't exactly sure what Todd was talking about a lot of the time. He used football phrases and expressions she'd never heard before, but she didn't dare ask what would certainly be dumb questions. She liked listening to the sound of his deep voice, even if nothing he said made sense.

The stadium parking lot was filling up fast when Todd pulled in. He got out, grabbed his gear out of the back of the truck, and came around to open the door for Stephanie.

"Hey, Cooper!" A huge, sandy-haired guy walked up to Todd and punched him playfully on the shoulder. "Ready for a tough game?" He glanced at Stephanie, nodding in approval. "Your mind's gonna be on the game and not on your date, right?"

"My mind is *always* on the game," Todd said, taking Stephanie's hand. "Stephanie, this is Ron Webb."

"And Elise," added the tall, attractive blonde approaching the group.

Ron grabbed Elise around the waist, gave her a quick kiss, then released her, turning his attention back to Todd. "I don't think much of the coach's special play. How about you and me talking to him about it while those junior varsity runts entertain the girls?"

Todd flashed Stephanie his best smile. "Save a seat. We won't be long."

"Right," Elise groaned, taking Stephanie by the arm. "The last time Ron left me for a talk with the coach, I sat by myself through the entire JV game. And the varsity game, too, of course, since he was playing."

Stephanie hadn't expected Todd to spend the whole evening glued to her side, but she assumed he'd want to stick around for at least the first fifteen minutes of their date. At this rate, she'd be spending more time with Elise than with Todd!

"Have you gone out with Todd before?" Elise shouted over the cheers of noisy Oakmont fans.

Stephanie shook her head.

"Ron and I have been going out off and on for nearly a year." Elise made a face. "Mostly off. Ron's cute, but he can be a jerk sometimes. . . ."

A loud horn blast signaled the end of the first half, and the JV team left the field.

"Finally!" Elise exclaimed. She stood up and waved wildly. "Up here, you two!" she shouted at Todd and Ron. They waved back and made their way up the bleachers.

When Stephanie moved her purse from the space she had reserved for Todd, one of the straps caught on the foot of the person in the row behind her.

"Sorry," she said, pulling the strap free. Looking up, she saw that the owner of the oversize tennis shoe was none other than Derek Gaines! Of course, he had every right to be at the football game just like anyone else, but sitting right behind her was too much.

"Great game," Derek commented, oblivious to the annoyed look on Stephanie's face.

"This is nothing compared to what's coming up when the *big guys* play," Todd said, sitting between Stephanie and Ron, with Elise at the far end.

Ron spoke up. "Hey, Stephanie, Todd tells me your family is really *interesting.*" She wanted to melt into her seat as he continued in a loud voice, "Like, all of you have names that begin with S."

"Even the dog's name is Spot!" Todd said as Ron roared.

"He *is* a dalmatian," Stephanie pointed out. But much to her embarrassment, that brought on even more laughter.

Todd put his arm around her and gave her a squeeze. "Stephanie's the sweetest Stockwell sister." He jabbed Ron in the ribs. "Try saying *that* one ten times in a row!"

Elise leaned across Ron, shaking her head. "Ignore them, Stephanie."

"You can take a joke, can't you, Steph?" Todd asked, grinning.

Stephanie nodded. She could take a joke with the best of them. She'd been teased about the "S-thing" before, only the teasing seemed different this time.

But Todd held her close, and as the second half began, she didn't even care what was happening around her. All she cared about was sitting close to Todd Cooper. Even when he told Elise about his unusual introduction to her family, his words barely penetrated Stephanie's rosy haze. She turned her head slightly, rubbing her cheek on the soft leather of Todd's jacket sleeve.

Unfortunately, he chose that exact moment to lunge out of his seat, shouting, "Come on, Johnson, get the lead out and tackle someone!" As Todd raised his arm from around Stephanie's shoulder, his class ring caught in the sleeve of her sweater. He tried unsnagging it, his eyes darting impatiently back and forth from the football field to the ring.

"Darn!" he muttered.

Stephanie sat very still, afraid that if she moved a muscle she'd lodge the ring even deeper into her sweater. "Actually," she said lightly, "this is more of an 'undarning' situation."

She knew immediately by the blank look on Todd's face that her attempt at humor had fallen totally flat.

From behind her, another hand appeared over Stephanie's shoulder. "Undarning is one of my specialties," Derek Gaines said as he bent over, his head only a few inches from Stephanie's startled face. A moment later Derek had deftly freed the ring. "There," he said, patting her shoulder. "No damage done."

"Hey, thanks," Todd acknowledged, double-checking his ring. "You're dangerous," he told Stephanie, "but cute." Then he turned his attention back to the game.

Stephanie tucked the loop of yarn back into her sweater and glanced over her shoulder, smiling at Derek. "You're right—no damage done. Thanks."

"Todd's right, too," Derek said.

"About my being dangerous?"

"About your being cute." He winked. "I guess you could call us the *Right* brothers, huh?"

Stephanie groaned at his pun and turned back around to watch the game. Imagine that! Derek the Spy actually had a good sense of humor!

For the next half hour, Todd diligently explained every play of the JV game to Stephanie. But her brain was saturated with football information after just ten minutes. While Todd did his sports commentary, Stephanie concentrated on the sound of his voice and the color of his eyes. She just smiled and nodded as if she understood everything he said.

When the fourth quarter started, Ron

slapped Todd on the back. "Come on, buddy. Time to show these folks how the game should be played."

Todd stood up. "We'll meet you girls in the gym later," he said. With a parting smile and a wink to Stephanie, he was gone.

Elise moved next to her. "So, are you a football expert yet?"

"Definitely," Stephanie answered, grinning. "Three strikes and you're out, right?"

Chapter Four

When the varsity team trotted onto the field, Stephanie picked Todd out right away—number sixteen. She was glad she knew his number, since the players looked alike in all that padding.

"Which one is Ron?" Stephanie asked Elise.

They had moved to seats closer to the field, leaving Derek Gaines to breathe down someone else's neck.

"Lucky number seven, leading the warm-up exercises."

Stephanie watched Ron guide the Cougars through some calisthenics and stretches. Once the game started, both girls jumped up and down constantly, cheering wildly when Todd or Ron was involved in a play. The game ended with a Cougar victory.

"You'd better prepare yourself," Elise warned as they made their way out of the stadium.

Stephanie wasn't sure what she meant. "For the dance?"

"For more football talk. If we're lucky, we'll dance once or twice." Elise didn't sound very enthusiastic.

Stephanie and Elise were swept up in the stream of Oakmont students heading for the gym, where couples were already dancing. Stephanie loved to dance, and she hoped that maybe Elise was wrong about the guys being more interested in talking about the game with their teammates.

She spotted Derek Gaines leading Bonnie Kramer, the Collegiennes president, out onto the dance floor. The tempo was fast, and Stephanie was surprised to see how well Derek danced. "I see some other lonesome football-player dates over there," Elise said, pointing to a group of girls sitting in a section of bleachers on the other side of the gym.

She and Stephanie walked around the dance floor and joined the other girls. Elise introduced Stephanie to the ones she didn't already know, adding, "Stephanie is Todd Cooper's date."

"We were wondering who he'd come with," a girl named Melanie said. She turned to the girl next to her. "Christine, you hear everything. What happened with Ashley, anyway?"

"I heard that she went out with Kyle Mason a few times while she was dating Todd," Christine eagerly informed the group. Most of the girls gasped. "Todd was *furious.*"

"And jealous, I'll bet," Melanie added.

"His heart mended in record time," Elise pointed out. "Right, Stephanie?"

"Yeah. Sure." Stephanie responded, wishing she felt a little more self-assured. She only half listened to the rest of the conversation about Todd's previous girl-friends, which Elise politely ended soon enough. Stephanie was getting a funny feeling about tonight's date. *Had Todd asked her out only to spite Ashley for seeing Kyle Mason?*

Her thoughts were interrupted when some-one tapped her shoulder. "Want to dance?"

It was Derek Gaines. Stephanie hesitated for a moment. None of the other football players' dates were dancing. Was there an unwritten rule that Elise hadn't told her about? Well, if there was, she didn't care. She followed Derek onto the gym floor, and they began dancing to one of her favorite fast songs.

Every time Stephanie looked up, Derek was smiling at her. She was still amazed at how well he danced. Obviously he didn't spend *all* his time studying.

When the fast song ended, a slow one started. Instead of walking Stephanie back to the bleachers, Derek took her hand.

"I love this song," he admitted. One arm reached around her waist, drawing her closer, while his other hand gently held hers against his shoulder.

"Me, too," Stephanie agreed, amazed that they had similar music tastes. She shook her head slightly. Missy wasn't going to believe any of this!

"What's the matter?" Derek asked, looking down at her.

Stephanie smiled. "Nothing. You're a terrific dancer."

"You're surprised?"

Shocked was a better description! "Well . . ."

But before Stephanie could finish her sentence, Todd's voice intruded. "Time's up, buddy." He took Stephanie's hand out of Derek's, and seeming quite full of himself, announced, "She's with me."

He whisked Stephanie away before she had a chance to thank Derek for the dance. Todd wrapped both of her arms around his neck and secured his around her waist. Stephanie's fingers touched Todd's hair, still damp from the shower, and she closed her eyes, quickly forgetting how much she enjoyed dancing with Derek.

I've died and gone to heaven, she thought, inhaling Todd's terrific cologne.

The song ended far too soon. Todd and Stephanie joined Ron and Elise and two other couples near the snack bar, and immediately the football talk began.

Elise gave Stephanie an I-told-you-so look before saying, "I usually give Ron fifteen minutes before I start bugging him to dance."

Todd put his arm around Stephanie's waist as another couple approached the group. It was Ashley and Kyle. *They look like Barbie and Ken,* Stephanie thought. Ashley was a gorgeous blonde, complemented by handsome, dark-haired Kyle.

"Hi, Todd," Ashley said sweetly. "You know Kyle, don't you?" She studied Stephanie with interest. "And this is . . ."

"Stephanie," Todd filled in. He held Stephanie closer and nuzzled her ear. "Come on—let's dance."

Elise examined her watch. "This is a record!" she gasped. "Only eleven minutes of game-talk! Let's dance, too, Ron." She tugged on his arm.

Todd and Stephanie again joined the crush of Oakmont students dancing to the fast beat, but Todd seemed preoccupied. Whenever Stephanie looked at him, he was staring in another direction. She followed his gaze directly to where Ashley and Kyle were dancing. Catching his eye, Ashley bestowed a radiant smile on Todd.

Stephanie's eyes narrowed when Todd responded with a spectacular smile of his own. She'd bet a year's allowance that she and Kyle had nothing to do with the sparks igniting around their dates.

When the music stopped, Todd left a mortified Stephanie standing alone while he joined Kyle and Ashley.

A moment later, Kyle headed straight for Stephanie. Todd had apparently suggested he dance with her since Todd had taken over as Ashley's partner. What nerve!

Then suddenly Derek Gaines appeared

beside her. "You owe me the rest of our interrupted dance."

"Consider me gone for good, Todd Cooper," Stephanie muttered under her breath. With no hesitation, she stepped into Derek's arms and said, "Another perfectly timed rescue!"

Derek whirled Stephanie away from Kyle in a move right out of an old Fred Astaire-Ginger Rogers movie. "I thought you knew." He looked at her in mock seriousness. "I'm majoring in damsels in distress."

Stephanie giggled, her mood lightening instantly at Derek's silliness. She grinned at him and tilted her head back. "From now on, I'll always think of you as my knight in shining armor."

"In an average week, about how many times do you need rescuing?" Derek asked.

"I know this is hard to believe, but until the other day, when my foot accidentally got stuck in Todd's gym bag, I'd *never* needed rescuing," Stephanie told him.

"I guess that makes Todd an 'opening knight,'" Derek quipped.

They both broke up. A few people gave them curious glances, including Todd and Ashley, and Stephanie could have sworn that Todd was frowning. What was he dis-approving of now? Changing partners had been his idea.

"I have a feeling that 'closing knight' is more like it," she confessed to Derek.

"Problems?"

Stephanie nodded. "From the minute Todd rang the doorbell tonight."

Derek's expression grew serious. "I over-heard bits and pieces during the JV game before the ring incident."

Stephanie sighed. "I'm sure the entire stadium heard."

Derek smiled sympathetically. "Not the *entire* stadium. Maybe one or two thou-sand people, but not *everybody*."

"Thanks, Derek," Stephanie joked. "You sure have a weird way of cheering me up."

"Nine out of ten doctors agree that laugh-ter really *is* the best medicine," Derek declared.

Their dance ended with both of them laughing. Kyle joined them immediately, smiling apologetically. "I think Todd and Ashley are waiting for us over there," he said to Stephanie, pointing to the bleachers.

"See you later, Stephanie," Derek said.

Stephanie smiled. "Thanks for the laugh-a-minute dance. I may never recover!"

Todd and Ashley didn't seem particularly

pleased when Stephanie and Kyle sat down next to them. As soon as a new song began, Kyle grabbed Ashley and pulled her onto the gym floor while Todd watched glumly and Stephanie fumed. She'd tried being a good sport about the whole thing, but her patience was gone. She spoke Todd's name twice before getting his attention. Assuming that he had forgotten her father's Cinderella routine, she said, "Did I mention that my curfew is ten forty-five?" She was ending this date as soon as possible.

"You've got to be kidding!" Todd looked at the gym clock. "That's in fifteen minutes!"

"How time flies when you're having fun," Stephanie remarked dryly. She noticed Todd's jaw clench, and felt great satisfaction. If anyone's jaw should be clenched, it should be her own! Todd had just used her to make Ashley jealous, and she didn't like it one bit.

As a matter of fact, she decided she didn't like Todd one bit, either. He'd made fun of her family, abandoned her three times, and, during what little time they were together, centered the conversation around his two favorite subjects—himself and football. All of this in one short evening! By now Stephanie Stockwell was an expert on Todd Cooper, but Todd Cooper knew absolutely nothing about Stephanie Stockwell.

Only the fact that Todd had chosen her to make Ashley jealous made Stephanie feel a little better. On the date scale, that brought tonight's rating up to a one.

Except for the music from the tape player, the ride home was silent. When Todd walked Stephanie to her front door, he looked around nervously.

"Is something wrong?" Stephanie asked, breaking the uncomfortable silence.

"It's ten to eleven," Todd said. "I was half expecting your father to attack me with a samurai sword or something."

Stephanie wished that he would. "Thanks for a nice evening, Todd," she said, opening the door. "I enjoyed meeting some of your friends." She was proud of herself for having come up with that gracious truth.

Todd gave Stephanie a quick kiss on the cheek. "We'll do it again sometime."

"Over my dead body!" Stephanie whispered as she watched him rush back to his truck. As he drove off, she cupped her hands around her mouth, loudspeaker-style, and yelled, "I hope you get a speeding ticket on your way back to the dance!" She was sure that's where he was headed.

Stephanie closed the door silently behind her, thinking that Todd would be astonished if he knew that the highlight of Stephanie's evening had been Derek "the Spy" Gaines. In fact, she was having a hard time accepting that herself.

Chapter Five

At ten o'clock the next morning, Stephanie squinted at the clock on her nightstand, then moaned and pulled the covers over her head.

The pounding on the door continued. "We know you're awake, Steph, and we're coming in," one of the twins threatened.

True to their word, Sarah and Shannon barged in, flopping down on either side of their sister.

"We finished writing the play," Sarah announced proudly.

"Mom's getting the stuff we need for costumes," Shannon continued. "We can start rehearsing as soon as our witch gets up. The show's tomorrow, you know." She started tickling Stephanie, who screeched and wriggled away, right into Sarah's waiting fingers.

From the doorway, Mrs. Stockwell shouted over the shrieking, "Stephanie! Telephone. Take it in my bedroom."

"Time out!" Stephanie gasped. She jumped off the end of the bed with Sarah still attached. "Is this any way to treat the star of your play?"

Shannon looked at Stephanie in disbelief. "The star? Since when is a witch the star?"

Sarah released her. "The *princesses* are always the stars."

"And you two are the princesses, of course," Stephanie said, grabbing her bathrobe.

"Of course," the two said matter-of-factly.

Stephanie ran across the hall to her parents' room and picked up the phone. "Hello?"

"Hi, Stephanie," a female voice said. "This is Bonnie Kramer from the Collegiennes. I'm calling about your tutoring assignment."

Stephanie found a notebook and pen in the drawer of her mother's bedside table. "Hi."

"Your student is Eddie Newman. He's eight years old," Bonnie told her. "His parents are divorced. His father lives in Ohio and doesn't keep in touch. Eddie lives with his mother, who works two jobs to make ends meet. She doesn't have much spare time to help Eddie with schoolwork. Right now he's a third grader reading at a first-grade level."

Stephanie's heart went out to the little boy.

"You can arrange your tutoring sessions with Mrs. Newman," Bonnie continued. She gave Stephanie the Newmans' phone number. "If there are any problems, just let me, or any Collegienne, know how we can help."

"Thanks, Bonnie," Stephanie said. "I'm embarrassed to admit that I'm a little nervous."

"We all feel that way when we meet new students," Bonnie assured her. "When you and Eddie get together, you'll relax. If you call Mrs. Newman today, you can schedule your first session for next week."

After the phone call, Stephanie went back to her own room to get dressed. She then went downstairs. Mrs. Stockwell was sitting at the dining room table sewing costumes for the play. "How'd your date go last night, honey?" Mrs. Stockwell asked, looking up at Stephanie.

Stephanie wrinkled her nose. "Not so great." She gave her mother a brief rundown, deliberately leaving out the times Todd had ridiculed the family.

Sarah burst into the room just as Stephanie finished. "Finally!" she exclaimed. "Dad's got the set ready, Steph." She slapped several sheets of lined paper in front of Stephanie. "Rehearsal in five minutes!"

"Slave driver!" Stephanie muttered, picking up the handwritten script. She read a few lines and started giggling. "This is classic Stockwell," she told her mother. "You'd better reserve a front-row seat!"

An hour later, Stephanie escaped rehearsal and went to the kitchen, where her mother was feeding Stacey.

"Hi, Stacey," Stephanie said, sitting on the stool beside her baby sister.

Stacey shrieked in terror and hid her face with her bib.

"What's the matter?" Stephanie asked, surprised by her sister's reaction.

Mrs. Stockwell took Stacey in her arms, smiling. "The answer's as plain as the *nose* on your face."

Stephanie caught sight of her reflection in the kitchen window. She had forgotten about the black clay wart on the side of her nose and the three short pieces of pipe cleaner the twins had added for "hair."

No wonder Stacey was frightened, Stephanie thought, taking off the wart. The thing was gross, all right!

"Any better?" Stephanie asked, and was rewarded with a smile from Stacey. She gave Stacey a kiss and turned to her mother. "I got my tutoring assignment from the Collegiennes this morning. His name is Eddie Newman. I'm going to set up a schedule with his mother, so if the twins want me for more rehearsals, tell them I moved to Alaska or something."

In the family room, Stephanie dialed the Newmans' number. On the third ring, a young voice answered.

"Hello?"

"Hi! May I speak to Mrs. Newman, please?"

"She can't come to the phone right now."

Stephanie knew that kids often said their parents were unavailable rather than tell anyone they were alone. So she asked, "is this Eddie?"

"Yes," came the cautious reply.

"Eddie, this is Stephanie Stockwell. I'm your reading tutor," she explained. "I'm hoping you and I can get together this coming week."

"I'm supposed to tell you that I can meet you at the city library after school on Monday," Eddie announced. "That way Mom can pick me up on her way home from work."

Stephanie thought for a moment. If she took a bus downtown after school, maybe she could hitch a ride home with her dad. The library was a bit out of his way, but she was sure he wouldn't mind. "Okay, Eddie, I'll see you at the library on Monday," she said. "I'll meet you in the children's reading room as close to three-thirty as possible."

"What do you look like?" Eddie wanted to know.

"I have dark hair and brown eyes." Realizing that didn't sound very distinctive, she added, "You'll recognize me the second I walk into the room. I'll be the one wearing a big colorful hat."

"Uh—okay," Eddie said. "See you."

"Bye, Eddie." Stephanie had just written a note reminding herself to wear her hat on Monday when the twins found her, abruptly ending her free time. The rest of Saturday and much of Sunday morning were filled with more rehearsals, costume fittings, and decorating the garage.

Sunday afternoon show time arrived before Stephanie had a moment to relax. In her black witch costume, she peeked out at the audience from behind the beach-towel curtain her father had secured to one side of the stage. She was amazed at the number of kids filing into the garage.

Shannon gave Stephanie's shoulder a little push. "Break a leg," she whispered in the fine old show business tradition.

Stephanie went onstage. "The Stockwell Theater Group is proud to present *Nightmare on Birch Street,* written by Sarah and Shannon Stockwell, directed by Sarah and Shannon Stockwell. The princesses are played by Sarah and Shannon Stockwell. Also featured is yours truly, Stephanie Stockwell, as the witch."

The audience clapped and cheered as the twins joined Stephanie onstage. They curtsied and the play began.

Stephanie moved to one side, shouting to an offstage character, "I warned you about walking so close to my fence!" She pointed a crooked finger at the fictional culprit. "Take that!" she cackled merrily.

"Grizelda's doing it again." Princess Sarah shook her head sadly.

"We've got to do something or the whole town will be filled with toads," Princess Shannon warned. "She turns everyone into toads. She has a nasty temper, but no imagination."

Sarah shrugged. "That's because she never finished high school."

"Aha!" Shannon said, as if that explained everything.

"Why are you two snooping around my house?" A scowling Stephanie hobbled up to the twins. "Unless you're especially fond of warts and the color green, you'd better leave."

Sarah sighed. "Don't you ever get tired of being mean, Grizelda?"

"Ha!" was Stephanie's reply. "I *love* being mean! Don't you two ever get tired of being nice?"

"Never!" the princesses cried at the same time.

"Well, I may have to teach you that nice isn't always best." Stephanie pointed both index fingers at the twins, but they whipped out the magic wands they had hidden behind their backs.

"Nice *is* best," Shannon said, aiming her wand at Stephanie, who froze in midspell.

"You look a little pale, Grizelda," Sarah quipped, pointing her wand in Stephanie's direction, too. "Have a double whammy on us!"

Stephanie grabbed her throat and staggered toward the curtain, where she collapsed, leaving only her feet in view of the audience. Behind the curtain, she quickly covered her face with green stage makeup and glued the wart in place while the twins continued their dialogue. A moment later, Stephanie stumbled back onstage. The audience laughed and clapped. When a loud, masculine laugh rang out above the others, Stephanie peered into the crowd, horrified as her eyes settled on Derek Gaines. What in the world was *he* doing here? She stood rooted to the stage, wishing the twins' magic wands would make her disappear.

Sarah waved her hands in front of Stephanie's face. "I said, 'Once she gets a look at herself, she might come around,'" she repeated loudly.

Sarah's gesture broke Stephanie's eye contact with Derek. When she felt Shannon's sharp elbow in her ribs, she swallowed hard and tried to concentrate on her lines.

"What have you done?" she wailed, reaching out to the twins with green-gloved hands.

Sarah held a mirror up to Stephanie's face. "See for yourself!"

"Arghhh!" Stephanie gasped, truly cringing inside. "Change me back!"

"Not so fast," Shannon warned. "Last week you turned the paperboy into a toad because the paper made too much noise landing on your porch."

"And the week before that, Mr. Phillips smiled at you when you were in a bad mood," Sarah reminded her. "And now *he's* a toad."

"Even the principal of our school hops around and croaks!" Shannon held her hand up to her mouth and in an aside to the audience said, "Although some of us can live with that!"

"The list of your bad deeds goes on and on, Grizelda," Sarah pointed out. "You've turned Birch Street into Ribbet Lane."

Once again, Stephanie heard Derek's laughter. She wanted to pull the clay wart off her face, tear it in two, and stuff it in her ears to shut out the sound.

Stephanie hung her head low on her chest, racing through her lines. "Now I know how it feels to be a toad. Awful! Miserable! Horrible! *Please* change me back!"

After what seemed like an eternity, the princesses agreed to remove the spell. Stephanie fell to the floor once more as the twins hovered around, twirling their magic wands above her body.

Hidden from the audience's view, Stephanie removed the green goop from her face and the wart from her nose. When she stood up, looking like herself again, the audience cheered, and Stephanie saw Derek put his fingers to his mouth and let out an ear-piercing whistle.

"H-how can I ever repay you," she stammered, "for showing me the error of my ways?"

"Money would be nice," Sarah suggested.

But Shannon shook her head. "Our father, the great king of this land, taught us that kindness is reward enough."

Stephanie put an arm around each twin. "Your father is a wise man. He raised two very kind princesses. Do you think we can ever be friends?"

"Maybe, if you promise never to be mean again," Sarah said earnestly.

"Never," Stephanie pledged.

"Then we'll be your friends forever," Shannon and Sarah said together.

Stephanie looked out into the audience. "The end," she said sadly, taking her bows with the twins.

After Derek's surprise visit today, she knew just how appropriate those words were.

Chapter Six

While the audience rushed to the refreshment table, Stephanie pasted a smile on her face as Derek Gaines approached. "What are you doing here?" she asked.

"I volunteered to chauffeur my cousins." Derek waved to a boy and girl who were stuffing cookies into their mouths. "My aunt lives four blocks from here. When I heard about the Stockwell Theater, I figured you'd be involved somehow, so I couldn't resist coming by."

Stephanie wasn't sure which was worse, having her face green with makeup or red with embarrassment. Either way, she knew she looked hideous. Fidgeting self-consciously with her costume, she sat on the edge of the stage.

"You and your sisters were great, Stephanie," Derek said sincerely.

She stared at him. "Great?" she echoed.

"Great," he repeated. "I don't know many girls who'd go through all this for their younger sisters." With one forefinger he gently wiped a smudge of green off Stephanie's cheek, and she groaned inwardly, wondering how much other goop she'd left on her face.

"I'm not volunteering for any more plays unless I have script approval," she joked feebly.

Derek grinned. "After that award-winning performance, I think you should check out your competition."

Stephanie gave him a blank look. "Huh?"

"How about going to the movies with me this afternoon?"

Stephanie was speechless, surprised that he was still interested in her. "Sure," she finally answered.

"Great!" Derek said enthusiastically. "I'll take Jason and Wendy home, then I'll come back for you in about half an hour. There's a terrific matinee at the Village Cinema—if you like science fiction, that is."

Stephanie looked down at her costume, her composure returning. "You're asking a witch named Grizelda if she likes science fiction?" She pulled the fake wart out of her pocket. "I'm even getting kind of attached to this thing."

"I prefer you unattached," Derek said, suddenly serious. "You aren't still attached to Todd, are you?"

"No. Never was," Stephanie admitted honestly.

"Good!" Derek's smile seemed to light the room. "In that case, I'll be back for you in twenty minutes."

Wasting no time, Stephanie hurried to shower and get dressed before Derek returned. Though he had enjoyed her sisters' performance onstage, Stephanie was not going to jeopardize her relationship with Derek by immediately introducing him to her family. She couldn't risk a repeat of the disastrous first impression they had made on Todd. When the time was right, she promised herself, she'd find a gentle way of easing Derek into the Stockwell Circus.

A kelly-green sedan pulled into the driveway. Derek jumped out and opened the passenger door for Stephanie, smiling at her. "No more Grizelda, Steph?"

"Nope. She's gone forever," Stephanie said as she got into the car.

"My cousins thought the play was terrific," Derek commented as he backed out of the driveway. "They were impressed when I told them I was taking the witch to the movies."

Stephanie rolled her eyes. "They'll really be disappointed when you tell them I didn't wear black."

As Derek pulled into the Village Cinema parking lot, Stephanie looked at the marquee. *"Creature from the Ozone Layer,"* she read aloud. "I hope the twins don't know about this. It might give them some ideas for their next play, and guess who'd wind up playing the Creature!"

Derek shook his head. "Dating a witch is bad enough. I don't think I could handle anything from the ozone layer." He parked the car and they both got out.

"Where did you live before you moved to Oakmont?" Stephanie asked as they neared the theater. She knew already, from Missy's office-snooping, that he'd transferred from out of state.

"In Denver. My father died in an accident last year. The only family Mom has is her sister, Jason and Wendy's mother."

Something in Derek's voice told Stephanie that the pain of losing his father was still fresh. "I'm sorry, Derek. Do you have any brothers and sisters?"

He shook his head as he bought their tickets. "I'm one of those dreaded only children."

"Sounds like heaven to me!" Stephanie said, laughing.

At the snack bar, Derek bought a jumbo tub of popcorn and two sodas. They settled into their seats, and the feature started. Between Ozone Creature battles, Derek reached over and took Stephanie's hand.

"Trying to keep me out of the popcorn?" she teased.

Derk smiled broadly. "You saw right through my romantic move."

Stephanie returned Derek's smile, reveling in the warmth of his hand. By the time the last alien had been destroyed, she was comfortably snuggled into the arm Derek had eased around her shoulder during the final on-screen conflagration.

"Thanks for a fun afternoon," Stephanie said as they left the theater, holding hands.

Derek squeezed her hand. "I had fun, too."

They walked to the parking lot and got into Derek's car. When he started the engine, he turned toward Stephanie and asked, "Do you want to go to the school dance with me next Saturday?"

"I'll go with you on one condition," Stephanie answered, grateful that J. T. Dunlavey's mother had told her she wouldn't need her to baby-sit for the little monster that night.

"Condition?" Derek repeated.

"Promise not to mention anything *remotely* connected with football!"

Derek laughed. "Okay, I promise. No football talk." He crossed his heart. "Now, about the dance on Saturday night—I have a confession to make."

"Like you've already asked three other girls?" Stephanie teased.

"Nothing like that," Derek said, grinning. "The Chess Club is running the concession stand and a friend of mine asked me to help him out for a half-hour shift."

"That's not so bad," Stephanie said. "Helping you at the concession stand will be fun."

"Actually, I promised I'd bring along *two* people . . ." Derek paused before going on. "Do you think you could talk Missy into coming?"

"Missy's my best friend. Of course she'll come." *Or I'll disown her,* Stephanie added to herself.

Derek turned the car onto Birch Street. "By the way, I didn't have a chance to tell you—I finally got into that advanced chemistry class I've been waiting for, so it's good-bye Mr. Osterman and study hall."

Stephanie realized that she'd miss his spying.

"I work after school at Ingram's Hardware," Derek continued as he stopped the car in front of the Stockwell house. "But I'll call you, since we don't have any more classes together."

He started to get out of the car to walk her to the door, but Stephanie quickly stopped him. "It's okay—I can find my way from here. I do it all the time."

Derek hesitated. "Are you sure? Isn't there something in the book of chivalry about walking damsels to the castle door?"

Stephanie shook her head. "Not unless there's a monster in the moat, and we're fresh out of monsters." As she got out of the car, she said, "Thanks again for a fun afternoon, Derek."

"And thank *you* for leaving your wart at home. I'll call you during the week."

Stephanie floated toward the house, a dreamy smile lighting her face. Suddenly the front door opened and Shannon appeared, dragging a reluctant Spot on the end of a leash. "Missy's called about a hundred times. I think there's something wrong with her hearing." She tugged on Spot's leash. "She kept asking whoever answered the phone if we were *sure* you were out with *Derek Gaines.*"

When Stephanie punched in Missy's number a few minutes later, the phone managed only half a ring before Missy answered.

"Hi! I thought you weren't coming back until late tonight," Stephanie said, trying to sound casual.

"I've had at least *ten* anxiety attacks waiting to talk to you!" Missy squawked. "You and Derek the Spy? What about Todd the Terrific?"

"Todd the Toad is more like it," Stephanie said, settling into the sofa. She gave Missy a full account of the last forty-eight hours.

"I can't *believe* I missed all this," Missy groaned. "I'm not dreaming, am I? Derek Gaines is really an okay guy?"

"I had more fun in five minutes with Derek than I did with Todd during our entire date. Of course, Derek hasn't met the family yet. They were too much for Todd." Stephanie thought for a minute. "Maybe they're too much, period."

"Your family is great," Missy argued.

"You're prejudiced because you've known

them forever." Stephanie sighed, closing her eyes.

"There's got to be a guy who'll appreciate you and all the fun at your house," Missy said encouragingly.

"Derek has a great sense of humor . . ."

Missy made gagging noises. "I'm sorry, Steph, but I'm having a hard time thinking of Derek the Spy as Derek the Dancing Dream Date."

"That makes two of us!" Stephanie laughed. "By the way, how's your own sense of humor holding up?"

"Why?" Missy asked suspiciously.

"Well, my best friend in the world," Stephanie began, "Derek asked me to the dance on Saturday night. I said yes, even though he said we'd be helping the Chess Club with the concession stand. Then he said he needed another volunteer." She took a breath. "One of his friends is helping out, and he wondered if you . . ."

"What!" Missy gasped. "Like a blind date?"

"Derek asked if you wanted to *help out.* He didn't say anything about a date."

"Are you sure?"

"I'm positive. I told Derek that you wouldn't mind spending a measly thirty minutes off the dance floor."

Missy groaned. "Thirty minutes filling a

million cups of soda! When the half hour is over, you'll have Derek and all I'll have is sticky hands."

"Then you can grab some cute guy and he'll be stuck with you the rest of the night!" Stephanie quickly responded.

"Oh, Steph, wait a minute," Missy ordered. "Which club did you say had the concession?"

"The Chess Club," Stephanie answered.

Again Missy gagged into the phone. "Isn't being a nerd one of the requirements for joining that group?"

"Derek's not a nerd. Be open-minded," Stephanie admonished. "Remember you're doing this for a good cause. Me."

Missy chuckled. "Are you sure you don't have another best friend willing to sacrifice her valuable time for you and Derek Gaines?"

"I'm sure."

"I was afraid of that," Missy said with a sigh.

Chapter Seven

On Monday afternoon at three-thirty, Stephanie adjusted her hat as she entered the library. All the kids in the Children's Reading Room looked at her wide-eyed while she walked slowly up and down the aisles, but none of them approached her.

Stephanie sat down at an empty table. All the tables and chairs in the reading room were small and low, adding to her discomfort. As she pulled a small stack of books out of her backpack, a quiet voice asked, "Are you Stephanie?"

She looked up. "Eddie?"

The redheaded boy nodded. "My bus was late," he explained, staring at her hat.

Stephanie smiled and pulled the hat off. "We can just get to know each other first," Stephanie suggested. "I brought some books I liked when I was your age. You can borrow them if you want."

Eddie looked at the cover of the book Stephanie was holding. "Maybe."

"I have the whole Rowdy Phillips series." Stephanie handed Eddie two of the books. "He's a young cowboy living in California during the gold rush days. In this one, he saves his family's ranch from rustlers. And in this one, he discovers a hidden gold mine in the mountains."

Eddie flipped through the pages and frowned. "Looks hard."

"You'll be reading them before you know it," Stephanie said with confidence. "You'll be helping Rowdy save the ranch and who knows what else? Maybe you can give my sisters some ideas for a new play."

Eddie brightened. "What kind of plays do they write?"

"The kind with witches and warts." She laughed to herself as she described the twins' theatrical triumphs, and went on for a while about the rest of her family. When she finished, she said, "Now it's your turn, Eddie. Tell me about you, and school, and your family."

Eddie shifted in his chair. "School's okay. I

like math, but I don't like reading much." He smiled impishly. "That's why you're here."

Stephanie grinned at him. "Do you like sports?"

"I like baseball," Eddie said. "Maybe when I'm old enough for Little League, my mom won't be working so much. Then she can take me to the practices and the games."

Stephanie and Eddie spent their remaining time together planning for the next session. They talked comfortably, and when Stephanie looked at her watch she couldn't believe their time was up. "My dad's picking me up in a few minutes, Eddie. Next week I'll help you with your school reader, okay?" She gave Eddie a big wink. "I don't have to wear the hat again, do I? Think you'll recognize me without it?"

"I'll recognize you," Eddie said.

Stephanie put the books into her backpack. "Is your mom coming soon?"

"In about fifteen minutes," Eddie told her. "Her other job doesn't start until seven."

"Do you stay at home by yourself when your mother works at night?" Stephanie asked.

"The lady from the apartment next door checks on me," Eddie answered defensively. Stephanie guessed he was afraid of getting his mother into trouble by admitting that she left him alone.

She tore a piece of paper out of a small notebook in her purse and jotted down her phone number. "In case you can't make one of our sessions," she explained, handing it to Eddie. "Or if you need someone to talk to."

Eddie tucked the paper into his pants pocket. He didn't say anything, but he looked appreciative.

Through the library window, Stephanie caught a glimpse of her father's small blue sedan pulling up in front. "I have to go now, Eddie," she said, grabbing her backpack. "See you next week."

"See you," Eddie said and smiled shyly.

Stephanie settled into the front seat of the car and described her meeting with Eddie. When her father pulled the car into the driveway, Sarah stuck her head out the front door and shouted, "Phone, Steph! It's a *boy*!"

Stephanie raced into the house, grabbing the nearest phone. "I've got it!" she yelled.

"Hi, Stephanie," Derek said. "I'm on my break at work so I can't talk long. Is Missy helping us out at the concession stand on Saturday night?"

"She'll be there."

"Great. We'll stop by her house after I come by for you."

"No!" Stephanie exclaimed. "I mean, we'll both meet you there."

Derek didn't say anything for a minute. "Stephanie, it's no trouble for me to pick either of you up."

"Then you can pick me up at Missy's," Stephanie said, pleased with her quick thinking—until she remembered Missy saying she'd be a little late to the dance because it was her parents' anniversary, and they were all going out to dinner. "Uh, Derek. I forgot. I won't be at Missy's."

"Is everything okay? Have you changed your mind about the dance?" He sounded worried.

"No!" Stephanie cried again. "I *haven't* changed my mind." She smiled. "You're still my 'Saturday Knight' with a *K*."

Derek chuckled. "Okay! I'll pick you up at seven sharp at your place. But what about Missy?"

"Missy's getting a ride with her brother," Stephanie told him.

"Cool. Listen, I have to get back to work.

If I don't see you at school, I'll see you Saturday at seven."

"Okay. Bye, Derek." Stephanie planned to be ready and waiting at the curb by quarter to seven on Saturday night, or so she thought.

When Saturday evening arrived, Stephanie's plans were unintentionally sabotaged. The twins were giving Spot a bubble bath when she needed the bathroom, so she hurried into her parents' bathroom, only to find the shower dismantled. Her father had been fixing a leak until her mother reminded him about his promise to barbecue chicken for dinner.

Stephanie raced back to the other bathroom and pulled the plug over the twins' noisy objections, saying, "You can give the dog a bath later. He's not very dirty, anyway."

At that point, Spot leapt out of the tub and shook himself vigorously all over the three girls—and the dress Stephanie had hung on the back of the door, hoping to steam out the wrinkles while she took her shower. By the time she had bathed, fixed her hair and makeup, and decided on something else to wear, it was ten minutes to seven.

The doorbell rang. Stephanie's eyes widened in near panic, which quickly turned into full-fledged panic at the sound of Spot's frantic barking. She froze at the top of the stairs, overcome by a sense of déjà vu. Sarah was holding the door open for Derek, who was unsuccessfully trying to remove Spot's paws from his chest.

Shannon suddenly appeared with a spray bottle. "Get *down*, Spot," she ordered, punctuating her command with a few quick squirts of water. That did the trick. It also made Derek very wet.

Eager to sweep him out the door before anything else happened, Stephanie rushed down the stairs. "Hi!" she cried. "I'm ready. Let's . . ."

Before Derek could speak, Mr. Stockwell rushed in from the patio. "Shannon, I can't control the fire without Old Faithful," he said, pointing to the bottle his daughter held. Then he noticed Derek and extended his hand, which was encased in a large oven mitt. "Oh, hello. You must be Stephanie's new young man. I'm Stephanie's old father."

Stephanie wanted to fade into the wallpaper. How could she explain a grown man wearing swim goggles and a bright orange apron that said, "Where There's Smoke,

There's Dad"? Mr. Stockwell insisted that the goggles kept the smoke out of his eyes when he barbecued. More than once, Stephanie had told him he looked like a World War I aviator, but that only encouraged him.

Derek finally found his voice. "Derek Gaines."

"Gaines with a G, huh?" Mr. Stockwell shook his head, then smiled. "Come and meet Stephanie's mother."

As Derek followed Mr. Stockwell and the twins down the hall, Stephanie knew that even throwing herself on the floor in their path wouldn't prevent his meeting the rest of the family.

"Sweetheart," Stephanie's father said as he came into the living room, "this is Stephanie's latest admirer, Derek Gaines."

Mrs. Stockwell looked up and smiled. "Nice to meet you, Derek." She was sitting on the floor completely surrounded by cardboard boxes and stacks of what appeared to be trash.

"Same here," Derek finally said.

"And this is Stacey," Mrs. Stockwell pointed to the baby, who was sucking on her pacifier. "Stephanie tells us you moved here recently from Colorado."

Derek nodded. "Yes—after my dad died. My mom's sister lives here."

"I'm sorry to hear about your father. But it's good your mother is near her sister. Family ties are very important," Mr. Stockwell declared earnestly.

Sarah sidled up to her father, looking solemnly at Derek. "Derek's dad is in the Bahamas."

Derek stared at her as Stephanie latched on to his arm tightly.

"We'll be late for the dance," she said, propelling him toward the door. "I'll be home early." Most likely *very* early after what Derek had just been subjected to!

"Nice to meet you," Derek shouted back to the family as Stephanie dragged him out to his car.

As they drove to the school, Stephanie sat in silence, too embarrassed to say a word.

Derek didn't say anything for a while either. "What gave your sister the idea that my father was in the Bahamas?" he asked at last.

"That's Stockwellese for 'passed away,' " she said sighing, knowing how ridiculous the explanation sounded. "When the twins were really little, my parents used the expression 'gone to the Bahamas' instead of saying someone died, so they wouldn't be upset." She chanced a look at Derek. He was grinning from ear to ear. Too bad he wasn't getting a kick out of some especially witty remark she'd made instead of laughing at her family.

"What was your mother doing with all that . . . er . . ." Derek hesitated for a second. "*stuff* on the floor?"

At least he was trying to be diplomatic, which was more than she could say for Todd. "Mom's into coupons and refunding. It helps on the grocery bills."

"What's refunding?"

"Some companies give refunds for buying their products, so Mom saves labels and outer packaging. Whenever there's a rebate on something, she has the manufacturer's requirements filed in her 'cardboard jungle,' as Dad calls her boxes."

Derek asked, "Does your mom save much money? Seems like a lot of work."

Stephanie gave Derek another sidelong glance. Was he really interested or was he making fun, like Todd? It really didn't matter since he'd probably never ask her out again. "According to Mom, after scouring the supermarket ads, paying attention to specials, and using her coupons, she saves from ten to thirty percent every time she shops."

Derek was quiet for a minute. Then he mused aloud, "Your family certainly is unique."

Stephanie giggled nervously. "That's them in a nutshell." She cringed as soon as the word *nutshell* left her mouth, knowing she'd left herself wide open for one of Derek's outrageous puns.

He said nothing, but Stephanie saw a grin tugging at the corners of his mouth. She could just imagine what he was thinking.

Chapter Eight

Inside the gym, a hand tapped Stephanie's shoulder as she and Derek walked toward the snack bar.

"I was hoping I'd miss some concession duty," Missy grumbled, coming around to Stephanie's side. "But my parents picked the most efficient place in town for their anniversary dinner."

"Hi," Derek said. "Ready for a fun-filled thirty minutes behind the counter?"

Missy presented Derek with her best fake smile. "I've looked forward to this all week." She whispered in Stephanie's ear, "If any soda spills on my brand-new shoes, you'll owe me. Anything remotely resembling a blind date is triple the penalty."

"You are so suspicious!" Stephanie said. "Derek didn't mention any plans about making us a foursome."

Suddenly Missy gripped Stephanie's arm. "I recognize that back!" she gasped, pointing to the boy serving a couple of customers at the snack bar.

"That's my friend Simon," Derek said.

"Simon *Abercrombie?*" Missy asked weakly.

Derek nodded. "Do you know him?"

Stephanie answered for her, since Missy seemed incapable of speech. "Simon sat in front of Missy in algebra last year. She has all his shirts memorized, don't you, Missy?"

"Uh-huh," Missy mumbled, her eyes still riveted on Simon's back.

Stephanie nudged Missy through the snack-bar door Derek held open for them.

"Say hi to your eager recruits, Simon," Derek said.

Simon turned around, bumping a full cup of cola against Missy's arm. Stephanie groaned when she saw some splatter on Missy's shoes.

Simon grabbed a paper towel. "Hey, I'm really sorry!"

Missy took the towel out of Simon's hand. "No problem," she said lightly, bending down and blotting a shoe. "I don't really care about these old shoes, anyway."

Stephanie stifled a giggle as Missy took a stack of paper cups off a nearby shelf and continued cheerfully chatting away to Simon.

Derek noticed the grin on Stephanie's face. "What's so funny?"

"Missy was so afraid she'd get sticky, but she sure doesn't mind sticking around now that Simon's in the picture."

Derek laughed and put an arm around her. "I'm all in favor of sticking together. After the dance, maybe the four of us can go somewhere for a bite to eat."

Stephanie looked up into Derek's blue eyes. "I don't think I'll have any trouble talking Missy into it."

The music started, and before long, thirsty dancers formed a long line at the concession stand.

"Hey!" Ron shouted as he walked up to the counter. "It's Stephanie 'Sayonara' Stockwell!"

Stephanie's face turned to flames. Ron took the soda from her outstretched hand, grinning.

Todd appeared beside Ron. "Sssay, sssweetie!" he said, overemphasizing the S's. "We're thirsssty." He and Ron howled.

"Take this and ssssssplit," Derek hissed, handing Todd a cup of soda.

Stephanie watched Todd and Ron walk away, the knot in her stomach unraveling slightly.

"Ignore them, Stephanie," Derek told her, squeezing her hand. "They're really jerks."

Stephanie nodded, knowing he was right. Still, their ridicule had hurt. She mustered a weak smile and turned her attention back to the counter. This evening had started out badly, and it was getting worse by the moment.

For the rest of their snack-bar duty, Derek said very little. More than once Stephanie caught him looking at her in that old "Derek the Spy" way. By the time their replacements arrived, she was convinced that Derek was working on a plausible way to ditch her. Why would he want to spend the rest of the evening with the laughing-stock of Oakmont High?

Derek's voice interrupted her thoughts. "Want to dance?"

Well, apparently he hadn't decided to ditch her yet. As he led Stephanie onto the dance floor, Simon and Missy were close behind them.

Derek didn't give Stephanie a minute of

rest when they reached the floor. After several fast songs in a row, Stephanie was glad when she heard the slow tempo of the next one. Derek pulled her into his arms, linking his hands around her waist. Stephanie's arms encircled his neck, and their eyes locked. Waves of delight flooded Stephanie's senses as Derek moved closer. And then he kissed her.

In that instant, Stephanie realized she was falling in love with Derek Gaines. She rested her head against his shoulder, swaying dreamily to the music. When the next fast song started, Derek gave her an incredible smile and a quick kiss before he reluctantly released her.

The last dance of the evening was another slow tune. Stephanie loved being in Derek's embrace. She closed her eyes, wishing the song would go on forever.

Unfortunately, the final bars of soft music were interrupted by Simon and Missy's enthusiastic arrival.

"Steph," Missy said, "Simon doesn't believe that you and I devoured a Gargantuan all by ourselves."

Stephanie held up her right hand and pledged, "In fifth grade Missy and I choked down every last spoonful."

"What's a Gargantuan?" Derek asked.

"Twelve scoops of ice cream," Missy explained. "With a different topping on each flavor, and gallons of whipped cream!"

"Don't remind me!" Stephanie groaned. "We were so sick, we missed school the next day."

Missy laughed. "Including the auditions for the spring play."

"Everyone who missed auditions ended up being trees," Stephanie remembered.

"I hope the moral of this story isn't that you hate the sight of ice cream," Simon said. "I thought it'd be fun if the four of us went to the Ice Cream Palace for a treat."

Missy took Simon by the arm, directing him toward the door. "You think a little thing like a hundred pounds of ice cream and miscellaneous toppings would keep us away from the Ice Cream Palace?"

Apprehension fluttered through Stephanie. She hadn't been able to eat ice cream since the Gargantuan episode, and Missy knew it.

On the way to Derek's car, Stephanie caught a glimpse of Ashley getting into Todd's truck. Todd's sarcastic words from earlier in the evening echoed in her ears, and she clenched her fists and willed herself to calm down.

A small white sedan pulled up beside

them. Simon's head poked out of the driver's window. "These girls want to ride in style, Gaines. Hop in. We'll pick up the Green Machine later."

When they got to the Ice Cream Palace, Stephanie's stomach lurched. She whispered to Missy, "I was hoping the place would be so crowded we'd go somewhere else—like the House of Tacos or Pizza Heaven."

"Come on, Steph. You can handle half an hour, can't you? Just don't eat anything," Missy whispered back.

"I'll have a hot fudge sundae," Derek announced after studying the menu.

"A triple banana split for me," Simon ordered.

Stephanie felt herself turning green, even without her witch's makeup. "Uh . . . just a glass of water for me, please."

"Two scoops of chocolate frozen yogurt in a cup," Missy told the boy behind the counter. They found an empty booth while Derek and Simon waited for their orders.

Stephanie rested her head against the back of the booth. "As soon as we walked in the door, the jinx of the Gargantuan struck."

Derek sat down next to her with his sundae, setting a large glass of ice water in front of her. Simon slid in next to Missy. "What jinx?" he asked.

"The one left over from our Gargantuan adventure," Missy told him. "I seem to be immune, but Steph can't seem to shake it."

"It's nothing, really." She took a sip of water. "It's just that sometimes I get a little queasy around ice cream."

Derek put his hand over his dish, shielding his hot fudge sundae from Stephanie's eyes. "Is this bothering you?"

"I'm okay as long as someone else is doing the eating," Stephanie said, not quite truthfully. She smiled faintly. "Pretty goofy, huh?"

Derek put an arm around her shoulder, and that made her feel better. Not good, but better.

As he finished his banana split, Simon said to Missy, "You don't have any pizza or hamburger jinxes following you around, do you?"

Missy thought for a moment. "I'm nauseated by too much homework, but I never met a food I didn't like."

Simon laughed. "That's a relief!"

"Simon's an eating machine," Derek said, eyeing his friend good-naturedly.

They spent the next hour laughing and talking easily. "Maybe we can all go for burgers next time," Simon stated as they headed for the door. At the prospect of a "next time," Missy lit up.

Derek shook his head regretfully. "Sorry— Mr. Ingram's doing a quarterly inventory at the hardware store, starting Monday. I'll be putting in a lot of extra hours, so count me out of any burger plans for a while."

"Call Stephanie when you're finished with inventory, Derek," Missy said. "She has a pretty busy schedule, too. J.T. Dunlavey and Eddie Newman are keeping her calendar filled these days, so I hope you two can find a time when you're both free."

Next to her, Stephanie felt Derek suddenly stiffen. She searched his face for a clue, but his expression was unreadable. *What's wrong?* she wondered as she got into Simon's car. Did the idea of a future date with her upset him so much? Until now, he had acted as if he really liked her. He had even seemed to take her oddball family in stride. What had happened to change his mind? Did girls who got sick at the sight of ice cream turn him off?

Simon put a tape into the cassette player and pulled out into traffic. "We'll drop Missy and Stephanie off first," he said to Derek. "Then I'll drive you back to school so you can pick up the Green Machine."

Stephanie hoped that Derek would say that he'd take her home, but he didn't. In fact, he hardly said another word on the drive to her house. While Simon and Missy waited in the car, Derek walked Stephanie to her door.

"Thanks for coming to the dance with me," he said, politely but formally. "And for helping out at the snack bar."

"I had a wonderful time, Derek." Stephanie's heart pounded especially fast. Was he going to kiss her goodnight?

He didn't. He just said, "I'll call you," then turned and loped back to Simon's car.

"Bye," Stephanie murmured. Disappointed and perplexed, she gazed after him through tear-dimmed eyes. Was this goodbye forever?

Chapter Nine

Late Sunday afternoon at Missy's house, Stephanie took a sip of the soda Missy handed her and settled down on her friend's bed.

"So," Missy said, her eyes sparkling with curiosity, "give me all the details. What did Derek say when he walked you to the door?"

Stephanie avoided her eyes. "He said he'd call."

"You don't sound very hopeful."

"After meeting my family in their natural state of peculiarity, followed by me nearly throwing up at the Ice Cream Palace, I don't think I'm on Derek's list of dream dates." Stephanie sighed. "I guess it's all too much for a normal person to handle."

"Stephanie," Missy scolded. "How many times do I have to remind you that your family is terrific? They're a riot!"

"That's because you have a warped sense of humor."

"Trust me," Missy insisted. "Derek really likes you, I can tell. A few unusual incidents aren't going to put him off."

"*One* incident was enough for Todd."

Missy sighed. "I thought we agreed you're better off without Todd the Toad. He doesn't have a single funny bone in his entire body."

"I'll bet Derek imagines me wandering through the house like Dad, wearing swim goggles and putting out fires with spray bottles," Stephanie said. "He probably suspects weirdness is hereditary."

Missy started laughing. "You're nuts!"

"Aha!" Stephanie exclaimed gloomily. "I rest my case."

"Stephanie!" Missy admonished. "My intuition says Derek Gaines will call you."

"Call me what?" Stephanie muttered. "I've decided not to help Mom with her garage sale next weekend," she then added.

Missy looked surprised. "Why? You love garage sales."

"I'm avoiding all public family appearances for a while. My love life has been

91

sabotaged enough." Changing the subject, Stephanie asked, "What about you and Simon? Did he ask you out?"

"I think so. . . ."

"What does that mean?"

"He asked if I wanted to go out for pizza," Missy said. "I said that sounded great, but he didn't mention any specific day or time."

"Was he too busy kissing you goodnight right about then?"

Missy pretended to look indignant. "You think I'm the kind of girl who kisses and tells her best friend?" She giggled. "Yes, that's when Simon kissed me." She hesitated. "I—uh—noticed that Derek didn't kiss *you*."

"Missy!" Stephanie wailed. "You were watching us?"

"True," Missy admitted.

Stephanie sighed deeply. "If Derek liked me as much as you say he does, he would have kissed me."

"Steph, this isn't like you," Missy said. "I hate seeing you so down. I want you to be as happy as I am."

"I'm not down," Stephanie insisted. "I'll be okay." Since she didn't want her mood spoiling Missy's day, she forced a smile.

"Did you learn anything important last night?"

"Hmm." Missy tapped one finger on her chin. "Helping your best friend's romance along is sometimes rewarding?"

Stephanie shook her head. "Being a nerd is *not* a requirement for membership in the Chess Club."

Missy grimaced. "Don't you dare tell Simon I said that!"

"Your secret is safe with me—until I need some good blackmail material," Stephanie joked. "I'd better go," she added, standing up. "I have to dig through the twins' room for some more books for Eddie. How's your tutoring going?"

"I'm meeting with Holly for the first time on Wednesday," Missy said. "Is Monday your regular day with Eddie?"

Stephanie nodded. "Yes. At the main library."

"I think Big Brother Chuck is doing research there all week. Since he'll be at the library anyway, maybe he can give you a ride home tomorrow and save your dad a trip."

Stephanie looked skeptical. "I know how Chuck feels about hauling us lesser humans around."

Missy ignored her. Sticking her head out

the bedroom door, "Hey, Chuck!" she yelled down the hall. "You're going to the library tomorrow, right?"

"Yeah," came the wary reply.

"Will you give Stephanie a ride home after her tutoring session?"

A few moments of silence were followed by another "Yeah."

"Thanks, Chuck," Stephanie shouted. "I'll be ready whenever you are." She turned to Missy. "What's with him?" she asked. "He's not actually nice these days, is he?"

"Ha!" Missy scoffed. "Mom calls it maturing, but I'm suspicious."

The first thing Stephanie did when she got home was check the message board in the kitchen, hoping that Derek might have phoned. She was disappointed to see only a note reminding her mother to put a garage sale ad in the newspaper. Wearily Stephanie trudged upstairs.

"I'm glad you're home, Stephanie," Mrs. Stockwell said. "I've tried to talk your father into putting the Horrible Hat into the garage sale." She lowered her voice to a whisper. "I didn't want to offend him completely by suggesting we put it on the 'Free' table. Maybe you can come up with a new angle because I was unsuccessful."

Stephanie chuckled. A new angle for the angler giving up his fishing hat? "I'll give it my best shot."

Inside her parents' room, Mr. Stockwell was rummaging through a stack of paperback books. When Stephanie walked in, she eyed the misshapen, faded hat perched on her father's head. What was left of the khaki fabric was held together by fishing lures of all shapes and sizes.

Before she could speak, Mr. Stockwell gave his head a vigorous shake. "This hat has character," he said, the clinking of spinners accompanying his words, "no matter what your mother says."

"We'll get you a nice *new* hat, dear," Mrs. Stockwell added as she joined them. "One that the fish won't laugh at."

"Well, maybe it has outlived its use," Mr. Stockwell conceded. "But I'm putting a high price on it, for sentimental reasons."

Mrs. Stockwell smiled, then turned to Stephanie. "Are you sure you can't help with the sale on Saturday?"

Stephanie avoided looking at her mother. "I have reports due in three classes." She wasn't lying, but the reports weren't due for two months.

Mr. Stockwell plopped the Horrible Hat on Stephanie's head, where it promptly slid down to her eyebrows. "A Stockwell garage sale won't be the same with one of the family missing."

Stephanie pushed the hat out of her eyes. "I'll work on the reports this week. If I have any spare time on Saturday, I'll pitch in." She handed the Horrible Hat back to her father. "By the way, Missy's brother, Chuck, is giving me a ride home from the library after I tutor Eddie tomorrow, so you won't have to pick me up."

Mr. Stockwell's eyebrows rose in surprise. "Chuck 'I-don't-do-anything-for-my-sister-or-her-friends' Franklin actually offered you a ride?"

"Missy asked him to—he's doing research at the library, so he won't be going out of his way," Stephanie told him, then left her parents and went into the twins' room.

Shannon and Sarah sat on the floor, sorting through piles of games and toys. As Stephanie stepped over the mess, making her way to the bookshelf on the far side of the room, Shannon screeched, "Don't touch a thing!"

"We haven't done the books yet," Sarah said, looking up from the notepad on her lap.

"I need a couple of books for Eddie's

tutoring session tomorrow." Stephanie pulled two books off the shelf.

Shannon wailed, "You're disorganizing us." She got up and took the books out of Stephanie's hand. "When we have our garage-sale pile and our keep pile, you can take what you want."

"Just one or two books?" Stephanie tried playing on their sympathies. "For poor little Eddie?"

Shannon shook her head. "Find one of Stacey's."

"Too babyish," Stephanie said. "Maybe I'll write one of my own."

"Hey! What a good idea," Sarah declared, suddenly brightening. "I'll help."

"Me, too," Shannon chimed in.

"Lending me a couple of your books right now would save us all a lot of time," Stephanie pointed out.

"But writing something for Eddie will be more fun," Sarah said eagerly.

Stephanie thought for a minute. "Actually, the book-writing project isn't a bad idea."

Before she could say another word, Sarah leapt up and grabbed another notepad off her cluttered desk. Thrusting it at Stephanie, she said, "You be the editor, Steph. You get to write."

"Gee, thanks." Stephanie sat down on the floor beside her sisters. "What about *The Stockwell Family in a Daring Rescue of Their Escaped Pet Hamsters, Lucy and Ethel*?"

"That's perfect," Shannon said enthusiastically. "I'll draw a picture of us hunting for Lucy and Ethel."

"And I'll draw us in all our plays," Sarah cried. She searched her desk until she found a set of colored pencils. "This is going to be great!"

"Yeah," Shannon agreed. "Do you think Dad'll make copies for us on his office machine? We can sell them at the garage sale and make a fortune."

Stephanie swore she saw dollar signs in both twins' eyes. "This isn't likely to make the best-seller list. This is for *Eddie*, remember?"

The twins grumbled in unison. But the thought of their lost fortune didn't dampen their spirits as they plunged into their artwork.

Stephanie was soon so caught up in her editorial work that she didn't even hear the telephone ring. But she did hear her mother calling, "Phone for you, Steph."

Stephanie raced into her parents' room, grabbing the receiver out of her mother's hand. "Hello?" she said breathlessly, hoping to hear Derek's voice.

"Stephanie?" a woman's voice said. "This is Mrs. Dunlavey. I'm taking a class this Tuesday and Wednesday, from four until seven. Can you babysit J.T. for me?"

"Oh, sure," Stephanie said, trying to hide her disappointment. "No problem. I don't have anything else to do."

"Thanks, Stephanie. See you Tuesday," Mrs. Dunlavey said and hung up.

Derek's handsome face appeared in Stephanie's mind as she put the phone down, but she forced herself to erase his image. From now on, she'd make sure she was too busy to dwell on Derek Gaines. By focusing her attention on Eddie and the monster J. T. Dunlavey, she'd forget him in no time. Then she closed her eyes, wondering how long "no time" was.

Chapter Ten

Eddie waved to Stephanie when she entered the Children's Reading Room at the library on Monday afternoon.

"You *did* recognize me without my hat," Stephanie teased as she sat in the empty chair beside him.

Eddie nodded, grinning slightly. He pulled a textbook out of his backpack and opened to the page marked by a baseball card. "Here's where I am in my reading group."

Stephanie noticed the first/second grade level printed on the spine of the book, though Eddie was in third grade. "Are you in the middle of this story?"

"We're almost done." Eddie sighed. "It's boring."

Stephanie moved her chair closer. "Let's

go back a few pages so I can get the idea of the story." Rereading familiar pages might give Eddie some confidence, she reasoned.

Eddie leafed unenthusiastically through the book, finally settling on a page, and began reading. Stephanie helped him sound out the many words he stumbled over. Often he glanced impatiently at the pictures above the text, guessing incorrectly at words.

"The drawings help us see the story better," Stephanie told Eddie, "but they don't take the place of the words." She tore a sheet of paper out of one of her notebooks, folded it, and covered the illustrated portion of Eddie's page. "I'll make you a deal."

Eddie looked suspicious. "What kind of a deal?"

"If you read the whole page without making a mistake, we'll put away your schoolbook and I'll show you a book my sisters and I made just for you."

"You *made* a book?" Eddie asked, obviously astonished.

"Not just *a* book," Stephanie said. "A *great* book. But first you have to read this page."

Twenty minutes later, both Stephanie and Eddie let out sighs of relief. He had read every word correctly.

"Good work, Eddie!" Stephanie praised.

He looked pleased with himself. "Finally!"

"Now for your prize." Stephanie set the book she and the twins had created in front of Eddie. Slowly and carefully, he read the bold black print on the bright yellow construction paper cover: "Art and all of the hard work by Sarah and Shannon Stockwell. Writing and editing by Stephanie Stockwell."

Eddie stumbled over the pronunciation of the names and wanted to know what "editing" meant. When Stephanie finished her explanation, he turned eagerly to the first page.

"Here's the Stockwell family . . ." Eddie read, then continued with the names printed below each sketch. "What's that thing on your dad's head?" he asked.

"A fishing hat," Stephanie told him. "A very *old* fishing hat." She studied the drawings. "Looks like the twins added some details after they showed me the pictures." She pointed to the snaggletoothed grin and beady eyes on the drawing of herself.

Eddie laughed and eagerly turned the page, reading aloud, " 'Which witch is which?' " The sketch showed beautifully dressed princesses Sarah and Shannon pushing ugly Witch Stephanie into an oven during their production of *Hansel and Gretel* last year.

The next page showed an unhappy witch face in the cutout oven door. "When they invited me for dinner, I didn't know I'd be the main course!" was written in a bubble above her head. The twins were bowing as the audience cheered, "Wonderful! Great! Terrific! Fantastic!"

Eddie's hearty laugh caused a few heads to turn around in the library. He moved on to the next page, a drawing of the Stockwells' two-story house, with a family member in every window. They were holding strange items in their hands.

" 'To find their escaped hamsters, Lucy and Ethel, the Stockwells gathered what they needed,' " Eddie read with Stephanie's help, " 'a fishnet, a jar of peanut butter, binoculars, an empty hamster cage, and a camera.' A camera?" Eddie repeated.

"Shannon thought the flash would scare Lucy and Ethel stiff so we could grab them."

"Did it work?"

"Turn the page," Stephanie suggested.

" 'During the whole hunt, no one noticed the most clever Stockwell of all.' "

The drawing showed all the Stockwells stalking around the living room, while in one corner little Stacey sat with a smug expression on her face and a very content pair of hamsters snuggled into the blanket on her lap.

Eddie howled. Stephanie smothered her own laughter and shushed Eddie. How would it look if a Collegienne and her student were kicked out of the library for disturbing the peace?

"One more page," she told him.

"Oh," Eddie said, obviously disappointed. "Is that all? This book is great! Can you make another one for next week?"

"How about you making one?" Stephanie said craftily.

Eddie looked away. "My family isn't funny."

"It doesn't have to be a funny book, Eddie," Stephanie told him. Was he worried about not having a father to include in his story? "How about writing a page about your best friend, and draw some of the things you've done together? Write about your neighbors or the kids at school."

Getting into the spirit of things, Eddie suggested, "How about my baseball card collection?"

"Perfect!" Stephanie agreed, putting a smile back on Eddie's face. She stood up for a second, peering through the doorway into the main room of the library where she'd spotted Chuck earlier. His notebooks were still scattered around the table, and he was at the desk, checking out research material.

Eddie flipped to the last page of Stephanie's book, which told the story of the annual Stockwell campout. The twins had captured last summer's trip perfectly. Near the campsite, Mr. Stockwell was fishing. The girls had drawn fish under the water, laughing and pointing at his ridiculous hat. The tent had collapsed with Stephanie inside. Sarah sat swatting mosquitoes, while Shannon nursed a bee-stung foot. Stacey played with an anthill, which sent the occupants in a straight trail to the campfire, where Mrs. Stockwell was burning something in a frying pan. In a bubble over her head was the sentence "Someday we'll look back on this and laugh."

Eddie closed the book. "My favorite part was the hamster hunt."

"Do you see how important the words are, Eddie? You'd never have figured out in a million years what was going on without reading the story," Stephanie said, stuffing the Stockwell saga back into her bag.

Eddie nodded. "Yeah. But most of the stories I read aren't as good as this one."

"That's what libraries are for," Stephanie said, gesturing around them. "They're filled with great stories. When your teacher thinks you're ready, I'll help you pick out some books about baseball players, or detectives, or astronauts, or cowboys—whatever you want."

Stephanie stood up again and grabbed her backpack. Chuck was walking toward her. "You did a good job reading today, Eddie," she said. "If you have any trouble making your book, call me and we'll work on it together."

"Thanks. See you next week," Eddie said.

Stephanie waved and left the room, meeting Chuck outside the door. "I'm all ready," she told him. Chuck, who wasn't known for his idle chatter, merely nodded.

They walked to the car, then rode silently home. The quiet didn't bother Stephanie. She was thinking how delighted she was with Eddie's progress. She might not be doing well in the romance department, but she was making a difference in one guy's life, even if he was only eight years old.

Chuck pulled up in front of her house. "Thanks a lot, Chuck. I really appreciate your bringing me home," Stephanie said as she got out.

"No problem," Chuck said, shifting the car into gear before driving away.

Stephanie was amazed that he hadn't made some crack about installing a taximeter.

Inside the house, Stephanie almost tripped over the boxes of garage-sale items stacked in the foyer.

"Did Eddie like our book?" Sarah asked, coming out of the kitchen.

"He *loved* it." Stephanie sidestepped the boxes and walked down the hallway. She smelled stew cooking.

"Dinner's in twenty minutes," Mrs. Stockwell said as she came in through the back door. "How about helping us drag these last few boxes out to the garage?"

Stephanie dropped her backpack on a chair and followed her mother back to the foyer.

"After dinner Dad's treating us to snow cones at Mr. Frosty's," Sarah said, picking up the smallest box in the stack.

Shannon chose the next smallest. "Mom says it's 'ice-cycle' night."

"It's *what* night?" Stephanie asked, hefting a large, heavy carton of toys.

"We're cycling for shaved ice," Mrs. Stockwell explained.

Inwardly, Stephanie groaned. Last month when the family had ridden their bikes to the park, they had all worn matching Donald Duck hats—Donald's beaks kept the sun out of their eyes, Mr. Stockwell had asserted. At the time it had been fun, but now it seemed crazy, though the rest of the family never questioned the sanity of Mr. Stockwell's suggestions.

No way was Stephanie going to go out again with a troop wearing or doing who knows what. What if by some quirk of fate Derek happened to see them? He'd think they were all completely nuts!

"I've got tons of homework," Stephanie said, lugging the box down the hall. "I think I'll stay home."

"Are you sure?" her mother asked.

Stephanie nodded. "Yes, I'm sure."

"Maybe she doesn't like us anymore," Sarah suggested.

Stephanie sighed. "I'm busy, that's all."

Opening the back door, Shannon commented, "You never used to be too busy for garage sales and bicycling."

"I've never been a sophomore with homework overload before." Stephanie carried her box into the garage and set it down near the others. *And,* she added silently to herself, *I've never had boys dropping out of sight at warp speed after meeting my family before, either.*

Later, from her bedroom window, Stephanie watched her family ride down the driveway, Stacey in a seat strapped to the back of her mother's bike. They didn't look *too* bizarre, she noted as they pedaled out of sight. Apparently visibility was the key word on this trip. Mrs. Stockwell was in canary-yellow from head to toe, while the rest of the crew were wearing fluorescent chartreuse, orange, and pink. She imagined Derek shielding his eyes as they passed.

Flopping down on her bed, Stephanie pushed thoughts of Derek aside and concentrated on how she was going to handle the rest of her life. From now on she'd only get involved in family projects inside the house. Anything that involved possible public access was out of the question, and that included the twins' future plays.

What about the annual campout? Stephanie wondered. *We're usually hours away from home. I'll be safe. Next year maybe I'll suggest a trip out-of-state.*

Stephanie rolled over onto her back and stared at the ceiling, picturing her family arriving at Mr. Frosty's, joking and laughing. Part of her wished she'd gone with them. But the more sensible part told her she'd made the right decision. So why the sudden craving for a root beer snow cone?

Chapter Eleven

Stephanie looked across the study hall table at the girl who sat in Derek's old seat, totally engrossed in *To Kill a Mockingbird*. She wasn't the least bit curious about what went on around her.

Missy slid a note under Stephanie's elbow. *Guess who I ran into a minute ago?*

If the stars in your eyes are a hint . . . Simon Abercrombie, Stephanie replied.

He asked if I'd have lunch with him tomorrow!

How can you? Stephanie returned. *Seniors have their lunch period before us.*

There's some special assembly so they have lunch early tomorrow. Isn't that great?

Stephanie stared at Missy's note. "Great"

didn't quite describe how she was feeling. It was obvious that Derek's lunch plans didn't include her.

Missy plucked her note out of Stephanie's hand and added, *Do you want us to save you a spot?*

Stephanie wrote, *To watch you and Simon make goo-goo eyes? No way! I've had it with romance.*

We do NOT make goo-goo eyes! came the reply. *And as for romance, what about 'The Spy'?*

Another victim of The Great Stockwell Curse, Stephanie wrote back.

Haven't you given up that ridiculous theory? Missy scribbled.

Stephanie shook her head and wrote, *Ridiculous? Then why are the only two men in my life Eddie Newman and J. T. Dunlavey?*

The bell rang. "I thought you were through baby-sitting J.T.," Missy said as they left the room.

"It seems I don't have anything better to do with my evenings," Stephanie sighed.

"But J. T. Dunlavey? Didn't you say his initials stand for Just Terrible?"

"It's been a while since I watched him. He must be two and a half now. Maybe he's matured. I'll call you later and give you the gory details," Stephanie said as she and Missy headed for their classes. "If I have the strength."

"J.T. has a little cold," Mrs. Dunlavey explained when Stephanie arrived at four. "You can make grilled cheese sandwiches and tomato soup for dinner—they're his favorites. There's chocolate cake for dessert." She opened the front door. "If there's a problem, you can reach Mr. Dunlavey at his office. The number's on the pad by the phone." She waved to Stephanie and left.

J.T. was lying on the couch in the living room, surrounded by stuffed animals and toys. He was absorbed in a cartoon on TV.

Stephanie sat on the end of the sofa. "Hi, J.T." He looked up, unsmiling, then stuck a thumb in his mouth and went back to watching TV.

Stephanie shrugged and reached for her backpack. The minute her back was turned, "*Nick!*" J.T. shrieked suddenly. "Want Nick!" He was standing on the couch, kicking off all the toys.

Stephanie sighed. "Who's Nick?"

"Nick!" he explained with two-year-old logic while he pounded his fists on the couch pillows.

Stephanie spied a red dinosaur under a

rocking chair. "Is this Nick?" she asked, picking it up.

"No!" J.T. screamed. "Want *Nick*." He started crying.

"Okay," Stephanie comforted. "We'll find Nick, whatever he is." She took the boy by the hand, and they began their hunt.

Every time Stephanie showed J.T. something she thought looked like the missing whatever-it-was, his hysteria increased. They spent nearly an hour searching. As much as Stephanie hated to bother Mr. Dunlavey at the office, she had no choice. She was sure that one more minute of J.T.'s squalling would result in permanent hearing loss. She'd just started dialing the phone when J.T. screeched even louder.

Stephanie slammed down the telephone and found him in the laundry room, pointing to a laundry basket on top of the dryer. Hanging over the edge was a piece of tattered flannel.

Stephanie pulled out the remains of a blanket. "Nick?"

J.T. snatched the scrap from Stephanie's hand and rubbed it against his cheek. "Nick," he cooed, marching back in to watch TV as if the last frantic sixty minutes hadn't existed.

Stephanie sighed deeply. "Why can't he

114

have a 'blankie' like every other kid?" She glanced at the clock. While J.T. was occupied, she'd get dinner ready.

"Come on, J.T.," Stephanie begged for the umpteenth time since she'd set supper in front of him.

The boy pursed his lips tightly and crossed his arms on his chest. " 'Loney."

"You mean baloney?" J.T. nodded enthusiastically. "But your mother said *this* was your favorite—"

J.T. knocked his grilled cheese sandwich onto the floor. So Stephanie made a baloney sandwich. J.T. took three eager bites, then shook his head. "Jelly!" he yelled.

"No," Stephanie said firmly. "You asked for baloney and baloney is what you got."

"Jelly!" J.T. started screaming at the top of his lungs.

Two jelly sandwiches and a jumbo piece of chocolate cake topped with whipped cream finally made him happy. Stephanie had a major headache and was overjoyed when Mrs. Dunlavey walked in a half hour ahead of schedule.

Mrs. Dunlavey patted the silent J.T. on the head. "Has he been a perfect angel while Mommy was gone?" She looked at Stephanie for a sign of agreement that she didn't give.

"I don't remember 'Nick,'" Stephanie said instead.

"Oh, yes. Somewhere along the way his 'night-night' blanket became Nick," Mrs. Dunlavey said vaguely as she walked Stephanie to the door. "I can't even wash it without his having a fit."

"I'll see you tomorrow," Stephanie said, and made her escape.

As soon as she got home, she checked the message board. Two notes were written in the twins' scrawly, identical handwriting. First, "Missy went to Gram's. Be home late. See you tomorrow."

Next, "Call Eddie. He thought our book was really terrific." That was followed by, "He didn't say the last part on his own. Shannon asked."

Stephanie wondered if she'd ever give up hoping to hear from Derek, and decided she probably wouldn't.

When she called Eddie, he hesitantly told her that he needed help writing his book. She agreed to meet him at his apartment on Friday afternoon after school.

Then Stephanie headed upstairs to a soothing, hot bath before she tackled her homework. She pretended each bubble was J.T. and swished every last one of them down the drain when she finished soaking.

*   *   *

At lunchtime the next day, Stephanie avoided the cafeteria. She found an empty table under the awning near the quad and had just taken a healthy bite out of her tuna and alfalfa sprout sandwich when Missy sat down on the bench across from her.

"We decided the fresh air would do us all good," Missy said, her smile impish.

Simon Abercrombie took the spot next to her, and Derek Gaines sat beside Stephanie. His gaze met hers briefly. "Hi."

Stephanie's heart thudded wildly at the sight of him. She tried to swallow and say hello at the same time, but choked on her sandwich instead.

Derek pounded her on the back. "Are you okay?"

"Fine," she croaked, gasping for breath.

Simon leaned across the table. "Grazing?" he asked.

Stephanie's hand flew to her lips and discovered dangling alfalfa sprouts. As gracefully as possible, she stuffed them back into her mouth. "I've always considered 'The Sound of Moo-sic' my theme song," she giggled uneasily.

Derek laughed. "I bet you like 'moo-seums,' too."

After a loud groan, Simon commented, "You two are a match made in a loony bin!"

"I've been telling Stephanie that for days," Missy told him. "Aren't they perfect together?"

In my dreams, Stephanie thought, double-checking for sprouts hanging off her chin. She looked into Derek's handsome face, seeing his blue eyes bright with humor. He'd probably be shocked if he knew how glad she was to see him again.

Stephanie cleared her throat, hoping that her voice wouldn't betray her nervousness. "How's inventory going at Ingram's Hardware, Derek?"

"Down to the nuts and bolts, as we say in the business," Derek said solemnly.

"Don't get him started, Stephanie," Simon begged.

"Simon and I are going for pizza after school on Friday. Do you two want to come?" Missy asked.

Stephanie shook her head. "I can't. I'm going over to Eddie's."

"You're spending way too much time with Eddie and J. T. Dunlavey, Steph," Missy said. "After two evenings in a row with J.T., you'll really need a pizza break."

Stephanie was about to say she'd call

Eddie and change their appointment to Saturday when Derek spoke up. "Sorry. I can't get away from the store." The coolness in his voice depressed Stephanie, and she noted that his expression matched his tone. Why had he even bothered coming over to her table?

"Well, with Simon around," Missy said, patting Simon's arm, "there'll be lots more chances for pizza."

Derek added, "And tacos, hamburgers, submarine sandwiches, and . . ."

"A Gargantuan at the Ice Cream Palace?" Missy supplied.

Simon put his arm around her shoulders. "We don't want to make Stephanie sick by dragging her there again," he teased.

"What was the senior meeting about?" Stephanie asked Derek, grasping for a subject safely away from the topic of ice cream.

"SATs, college applications, student loans . . ." Derek began, avoiding Stephanie's gaze.

". . . scholarships, grants, and senior pictures," Simon finished.

Stephanie took the last bite of her sandwich, carefully tucking all wayward sprouts into her mouth. "Where are you going to college, Derek?"

"JC," he answered.

"Santa Teresa Junior College?" Missy's eyes widened. "But that's only five miles away! With your grades you could go anywhere."

"My grades and a lot of money," Derek amended. He sounded matter-of-fact, not bitter or angry.

"What about scholarships and grants?" Stephanie asked.

Derek shook his head. "Not enough for four full years."

Simon stood up. "Derek's too cool to admit he'd be lost without me. I'm going to JC, too."

As the warning bell rang, Missy said, "See you in study hall, Steph."

Simon took Missy's hand. "Come on—I'll walk you to class. Bye, Stephanie. Catch you later, Derek."

Feeling awkward, Stephanie stood beside Derek watching Simon and Missy walk away hand in hand. Just then a tall blond girl playfully bumped Derek's shoulder.

"Chemistry notes," the blonde said, patting the binder in her hand.

"Great!" Derek exclaimed. "See you, Stephanie."

"Yeah—see you," Stephanie said flatly. Misery filled her heart as she watched Derek and the blonde leave the quad, wondering if Chem 120 was the only chemistry between them.

Two periods later, Stephanie passed her first note to Missy. *Was dragging Derek along at lunchtime today your idea?*

The only crime I'm guilty of is helping Cupid. Missy drew the initials *SS* and *DG* inside a heart pierced by an arrow.

I haven't seen or heard from Derek since the dance. Honestly, Missy, he's not interested in me, Stephanie scribbled.

Missy frowned. *Yes he is. When Simon mentioned double-dating to Derek, he said, "Good idea."*

Stephanie rolled her eyes. *That doesn't mean he was thinking about me! Give it up! There's no chance of our getting together.*

Derek likes you! There is no such thing as the Stockwell Curse!!! Missy tore a fresh sheet of paper from her binder. *If there really is a curse, why doesn't it strike J. T. Dunlavey?*

Stephanie wrote back, *At the rate I'm going, J.T. may be the highlight of the day!*

After school, Stephanie walked to the Dunlaveys'.

"Macaroni and cheese for dinner," Mrs. Dunlavey instructed as soon as Stephanie arrived. "Chocolate pudding for dessert."

Stephanie nodded and joined J.T. in

the living room. The welcome sight of Nick clutched tightly in the boy's hands greeted her. "One less problem tonight," she muttered.

Minutes later, J.T. stood in front of her, shouting at the top of his lungs, *"Macaroni!"*

Stephanie sighed. "Okay. Watch cartoons while I get your dinner ready." He nodded and flopped down on the floor in front of the TV.

Stephanie set the table while the macaroni boiled on the stove. She mixed the packaged ingredients and spooned J.T.'s portion into a bowl. "All ready, J.T." She went into the living room doorway and called again, "Dinner's . . ."

J.T. was still in front of the television where she'd left him a few minutes before, only now he was covered with black potting soil. He was methodically tearing apart a Boston fern that he had pulled out of its large ceramic pot.

Stephanie grabbed J.T. and Nick and carried them into the kitchen. "Eat your macaroni," she hissed after scrubbing the child and plopping him into his chair.

J.T. pointed to the refrigerator. "Pudding."

"After dinner," Stephanie said, searching for a broom. She'd sweep up the clumps of dirt while he ate, then vacuum.

She was patting the last bits of dirt around the repotted fern when J.T. yelled from the kitchen, "All done!"

The sound of the refrigerator door slamming sent Stephanie scurrying into the kitchen. J.T. was sitting on the floor with the serving bowl of pudding in his lap. He spotted Stephanie as he shoveled the first spoonful into his mouth.

"All done," he said with a big smile, indicating his empty plate. "Nick ate macaroni."

"What?" Stephanie frowned at J.T. "Nick doesn't have a mouth. He can't eat."

"He can, too." J.T. yanked on Nick, sending gooey macaroni and cheese flying all over the floor.

Stephanie closed her eyes and counted to ten. Twice. Her dream of romance had walked away with a blonde at his side and now this miserable brat was driving her out of her mind! The Dunlaveys would have to offer her twenty dollars an hour and a trip to Disneyland before she'd ever set foot in this house again!

Chapter Twelve

By the time Stephanie got home that evening, she was in a horrible mood. She thought about canceling her visit with Eddie, but as soon as she began to dial his phone number, she changed her mind and hung up. Eddie was looking forward to putting his book together, and no matter how dreadful she felt right now, she couldn't back out on her promise to help.

After school the next day, when she saw the excited look on Eddie's face, she was glad she hadn't stood him up. He was waiting on the sidewalk in front of his apartment building when Stephanie got off the bus.

"I already drew the pictures for my book," he said, leading the way to a small apartment on the first floor. "But I need help with the words. Mom's too tired to help me when she comes home from work."

Stephanie felt a twinge of sympathy as she heard the loneliness in Eddie's voice.

He guided Stephanie through the small, neat living room into the spotless kitchen. He pointed to some papers on the table. "My book," he said proudly. "Want a soda? And some cookies?"

"Yes to both," Stephanie answered. She sat down and looked through Eddie's work. "Let me guess on this one." Stephanie chuckled, holding up a drawing of herself.

"Pretty good, huh?" Eddie put their sodas and a bag of cookies on the table.

"Great," Stephanie answered. Looking at another drawing, she asked, "Who's this?"

Eddie flushed slightly. "My dad and his new family. I spent two weeks with them in the summer."

"Sounds like fun."

"It was okay," Eddie mumbled. "Only I wish they were more like your family."

The drawing showed two smiling adults, two smiling girls, and one solemn boy with red hair. "Alone in the crowd," Stephanie titled the picture in her mind. With all the chaos around the Stockwell house, she seldom had a chance to be alone. She found that oddly comforting.

"What do you want to write here?" Stephanie asked.

"Just names," Eddie said. He turned the page. "This is my best friend, Jake. We're catching lizards in an empty lot."

"Gross!"

He gave her a disgusted, you're-only-a-girl look and flipped to the next page. "This is what frog eggs look like." He'd drawn a hand holding a large grayish blob filled with tiny black dots.

"*Double* gross!"

Eddie laughed. "I only drew one other picture—me in a baseball uniform." He showed it to her. "That's how I'll look when I get on a team."

"The company my dad works for sponsors a Little League team in the spring," Stephanie told him. "Maybe one of the coaches could give you rides to practices and games when your mom is working."

Eddie's face lit up. "That'd be cool!"

"Now let's get back to work," Stephanie said.

For the next half hour, Stephanie spelled and sounded out the words for Eddie. He wiggled in his seat as he labored over each sentence. When he had finished, he let out a sigh of relief. "Whew! I'm glad that's done." He shoved the papers aside. "Want to see my baseball cards?"

Stephanie didn't have the heart to tell him all baseball cards looked alike to her. He'd worked so hard on his book that the least she could do was show interest in his favorite subject.

Eddie proudly set his enormous collection in front of Stephanie. While he chattered on and on about RBIs and HRs, she felt her brain becoming numb. Finally she interrupted, "You must be a genius if you understand all this stuff!"

He beamed. "Math's a cinch."

Stephanie laughed. "The next thing you know, you'll be tutoring *me* in my least favorite subject!" Suddenly an idea popped into her head. "We're having a garage sale tomorrow and math wizards are especially welcome, because my dad's the only one who can add. How about helping the twins with their lemonade stand?"

Eddie looked delighted, then disappointed. "Mom's working most of the day."

Stephanie hated the thought of more lonely drawings in Eddie's book. "Your mom could drop you off at our house. We'll drive you home after the sale."

"I'll ask," Eddie said excitedly. "I think it'll be okay."

Stephanie stood up. "I hope so. We're desperate for good help."

Eddie looked dubious. "With all the people in your family?"

"You can handle the cash box at the lemonade stand and referee the twins," Stephanie explained on her way out the door. "They argue about everything from the size of the serving cups to the color of the lemonade!"

Eddie laughed. "What's your job?"

"I—uh—I don't have one," she said. "I have other things to do."

"I'll call you," Eddie called after her. "Thanks a lot, Stephanie!"

Stephanie waved and hurried down the street to catch the bus. As she made her way to an empty seat, she smiled, thinking of the homemade pizza that would be waiting for her. Loaded with pepperoni, mushrooms, and gobs of melted cheese, her father's pizza was a treat the whole family loved. But instead of hunger, a pang of guilt pierced Stephanie. Eddie thought she was lucky to have such a happy, complete family. Maybe she was, even though they sometimes totally embarrassed her.

In that instant, Stephanie realized there was no way she'd be spending tomorrow inside doing homework while everyone else was outside having fun. She'd be the "bag lady" as usual, bagging all the great junk the customers bought.

Stephanie was feeling a lot better as she walked up Birch Street. But she stopped, rooted to the sidewalk, when she spotted Derek Gaines's Green Machine parked in front of her house. What was he doing there? More important, how long had he been there, unprotected from her family?

She rushed through the front door and peeked into the dining room, where she saw her mother sitting at the table. It was cluttered with her refunding stuff, and an unfamiliar dark-haired woman sat beside her, holding Stacey on her lap.

"Stephanie!" Mrs. Stockwell cried. "This is Delores Gaines, Derek's mother. I'm giving her a crash course in coupons and refunding."

For a moment Stephanie stared at them in astonishment. She'd assumed she'd find Derek, and instead, here was his mother! How did Mrs. Gaines and Mrs. Stockwell even know each other?

"Uh—nice to meet you," Stephanie told Mrs. Gaines when she finally recovered. Turning to her mother, she added, "Mom, I invited Eddie over to help with the garage sale tomorrow. And I don't have as much homework as I thought I'd have, so I'm helping, too."

Mrs. Stockwell stood up and gave Stephanie a hug. "That's terrific! Good bag ladies are hard to find."

Just then the twins burst out of the kitchen, their faces and hair covered with flour and their clothing dotted with lumps of dough.

"Dad fired us from dough duty!" Shannon announced.

Sarah picked a piece of dough off her shirt. "*You* started throwing first."

Shannon smiled. "It looks so easy when the guy in Bennicci's Pizza Parlor does it."

Mr. Stockwell, wrapped in a huge apron, followed the twins. There were traces of flour and dough in his hair, too. "Steph, as of now, you and Derek are in charge of the pizzas."

So Derek *was* here! But why . . . how . . . what in the world was going on?

Derek was sliding two large pizzas into the oven when Stephanie walked into the kitchen on rubbery legs. "Hi," he said casually. He was wearing Mr. Stockwell's "Kiss the Cook" apron, looking flushed either from the heat or from embarrassment. The oven door slipped out of his hand as he tried to close it, making it crash back open.

He grunted something Stephanie didn't hear, and shut it firmly.

She picked up a sponge with a trembling hand and started wiping flour off the floor and counters, thinking how cute Derek looked in her dad's apron. "So, what's going on?" she asked, hoping she sounded nonchalant.

Derek juggled two pot holders, avoiding Stephanie's eyes. "You mean why are my mom and I here? When I told her about your mother's money-saving techniques, she was really impressed." He leaned down briefly to peer into the oven window. "Our finances are pretty tight. My mother wanted more details about coupons and stuff, so she called your mother, and your mom invited us both over. And then she asked us to stay for dinner, which is how I wound up in the kitchen."

So much for his being unable to stay away from me, Stephanie thought dismally.

Derek leaned against the sink and folded his arms across his chest, dropping one of the pot holders in the process. As she picked it up, he said, "I didn't mean to show up on your doorstep just as you got back from your date."

Stephanie wasn't sure she had heard right. "Date? What date?"

131

"With Eddie. Remember him? The guy you said you were meeting today so you couldn't go out for pizza?" Derek regarded her closely, his eyes probing.

"But, Derek, Eddie is the little boy I tutor in reading!" Stephanie exclaimed. "He's eight years old!"

"Oh? Then what about J.T.?" Derek asked grimly. "Missy said he was taking up a lot of your time."

Suddenly everything began to fall into place for Stephanie. Derek thought she'd been dating other guys! Could he actually be jealous? The thought made her tingle all over. But to pay him back for causing her so much misery, she couldn't resist teasing him a little.

"J.T.'s a terrific guy," she said enthusiastically. "He's into screaming, unpotting plants, and hiding macaroni—when he's not getting all hysterical about losing an old blanket named Nick." She giggled at the stunned expression on Derek's face. Taking pity on him, she explained, "J.T. is a baby-sitter's two-year-old nightmare come true. Any more questions?"

Derek didn't smile. "Okay, so much for Eddie and J.T. How does Chuck Franklin figure in your social life?"

This time Stephanie was stunned.

"*Chuck?*" she gasped. "He doesn't figure in anybody's social life, certainly not in mine!"

"When I phoned on Monday . . ."

Stephanie stared at him. "You phoned?"

Derek nodded. "One of the twins said Chuck had just driven you home and you were outside talking to him."

"First of all, Chuck is Missy's uptight older brother. And second, he gave me a ride home from the library where I was tutoring Eddie, so I thanked him. That's it!" Stephanie tossed her sponge into the sink and took a dish towel out of a drawer. "I wonder which twin I'll strangle first for not giving me your message!"

"I didn't leave a message," Derek said, putting down the pot holders.

"Well, they could have told me someone phoned." Stephanie scowled. "I can hear their defense now!"

Derek started laughing. "Like how you didn't ask about phone *calls*, only phone *messages*?" He tugged on the end of the towel she was holding. "Does this mean you might be able to fit me into your busy social calendar?"

While Stephanie pretended to consider his question, Derek gave the towel another yank, pulling her closer.

"I thought you were studying chemistry with a tall, pretty blonde," she admitted, refusing to meet his eyes.

He cupped her chin in his hand and gently raised her face close to his. "Hillary's one of my lab partners," he told her, amused. "Her boyfriend is the other one."

"Oh," was all Stephanie could say, though she was glowing inside. Derek's expression was warm and caring. As his mouth curved into a sweet smile, she wondered why she'd never noticed the dimple in his chin before. Then she looked closer. Pizza sauce! She wiped it off his face and held her finger up for inspection, murmuring, "I can't resist a guy who wears *Eau de Tomato.*"

"You're pretty irresistible yourself," Derek whispered, his arms tightening around her waist. "I thought we had a good thing going between us until I heard about all the other guys you were involved with. I realized how much I really liked you, but I thought you were just playing the field, so I backed off."

"When I didn't hear from you, I was afraid you thought my family and I were overwhelming," Stephanie confided.

"I like your entire family," Derek said. "Including Spot." He looked down at the dog, who was industriously licking a blob of dough off his shoes. "I especially like you, Stephanie."

"You don't think that we're all crazy?" she persisted.

"If all the laughter around this house is caused by craziness, I'm all for it. It's the best medicine, remember?"

"You've convinced me," Stephanie admitted a moment before Derek kissed her. Pizza, dog, and family disappeared into the twilight zone as the magic of Derek's lips lingered softly on hers.

"It doesn't look like you two are keeping any eyes on those pizzas," Mr. Stockwell reprimanded jokingly from the doorway.

Derek didn't seem bothered by the intrusion as he released Stephanie. Mr. Stockwell laughed heartily and clapped Derek on the back. "This guy is okay, Steph." Then he gave Stephanie a quick kiss on the cheek. "Your mother tells me our garage sale will be a family affair after all. I'm glad."

"I'm glad, too, Dad," Stephanie said sincerely.

Mr. Stockwell left the kitchen muttering under his breath something about Gaines with a *G*. When he had gone, Derek said, "I have two small confessions to make before we rescue the pizzas and feed the starving masses." He cleared his throat. "The first is that I can read upside down."

Stephanie took a few moments to grasp his meaning. "You mean you read the notes Missy and I passed in study hall?"

"Not all of them," he confessed. "Sometimes your hand or a book covered what you'd written. But I did catch the part about Missy's liking Simon Abercrombie."

Stephanie's eyes narrowed. "Then you *were* spying on us!"

"Spying isn't the right word. Getting acquainted with you and Missy is a better way of looking at my . . . skill." Stephanie made a face, but he continued. "I don't think Missy and Simon mind my extraordinary talent," and Stephanie knew he was right.

"What's confession number two?"

Derek took hold of her hands, smiling. "I'm falling in love with you, Stephanie Stockwell."

"And I'm falling in love with you, too, Derek Gaines with a *G*," Stephanie murmured as Derek kissed her again.

Sweet Dreams

SWEET DREAMS are fresh, fun and exciting —alive with the flavor of the contemporary teen scene—the joy and doubt of first love. If you've missed any SWEET DREAMS titles, then you're missing out on your kind of stories, written about people like you!

❏	26976-3 P.S. I LOVE YOU #1, Barbara P. Conklin	$2.99
❏	28830-X PUPPY LOVE # 175, Carla Bracale	$2.95
❏	28840-7 WRONG-WAY ROMANCE #176	$2.95
	Sherri Cobb South	
❏	28862-8 THE TRUTH ABOUT LOVE #177	$2.95
	Laurie Lykken	
❏	28900-4 PROJECT BOYFRIEND #178	$2.95
❏	Stephanie St. Pierre	
❏	29021-5 OPPOSITES ATTRACT #180	$2.99
	Linda Joy Singleton	
❏	29059-2 TIME OUT FOR LOVE #181	$2.99
	June O'Connell	
❏	29290-0 FOCUS ON LOVE #185, Mandy Anson	$2.99
❏	29354-0 THAT CERTAIN FEELING #186	$2.99
	Sheri Cobb South	
❏	29449-0 FAIR WEATHER LOVE #187, Carla Bracale	$2.99
❏	29450-4 PLAY ME A LOVE SONG #188	
	Bette R. Hendapohl	$2.99
❏	29451-2 CHEATING HEART #189, Laurie Lykken	$2.99
❏	29452-0 ALMOST PERFECT #190	
	Linda Joy Singleton	$2.99
❏	29453-9 BACKSTAGE ROMANCE #191	
	June O'Connell	$2.99

Available at your local bookstore or use this page to order.

Bantam Books, Dept. SD 2451 S Wolf Road, Des Plaines, IL 60018

Please send me the items I have checked above. I am enclosing $_____ (please add $2.50 to cover postage and handling). Send check or money order, no cash or C.O.D.'s, please.

Mr/Ms._____

Address_____

City/State_____Zip_____

Please allow four to six weeks for delivery.
Prices and availability subject to change without notice.   SD 6/92